THE MYSTERY OF THE
WHISPERING WITCH

Trixie
Belden

Your TRIXIE BELDEN Library

Trixie
Belden and the
MYSTERY OF THE
WHISPERING WITCH

BY KATHRYN KENNY

Cover by Jack Wacker

GOLDEN PRESS

Western Publishing Company, Inc.

Racine, Wisconsin

CONTENTS

THE MYSTERY OF THE
WHISPERING WITCH

An Unexpected Visitor • 1

TRIXIE BELDEN GROANED and clutched her short, sandy curls with both hands. "Oh, woe!" she exclaimed. "Someone in Washington ought to pass a law about this, and if I had my way, they would."

Her best friend, Honey Wheeler, looked up from her English textbook and grinned. "What law do you want passed now?" she asked. "Wait, don't tell me. Let's see—last week you wanted to pass a law ending all chores for teen-agers forever, so it can't be that one again. A week ago, you wanted to pass a law about skirts. No one should ever have to wear one, you said, particularly Trixie Belden."

Trixie sighed. "I still like those ideas," she replied stubbornly, staring down with troubled blue eyes at her math book, which lay open on the kitchen table in front of her. "But *this* law would be about weekend homework."

"You mean you want *more* of it?" Honey asked, pretending to misunderstand.

Trixie made a face at her friend. "You know I didn't mean that! What I meant was that there shouldn't be *any*—especially on the weekend before Thanksgiving. Jeepers! It doesn't seem right, somehow."

Honey giggled and leaned back in her chair. "Let's face it, Trix. There really isn't any weekend that you and I like doing homework. Anyway, we've almost finished—at least, I have. I've only got one more paragraph to write for my English composition. How are you coming with your math?"

Trixie groaned again. "Terribly!" she exclaimed. "It's true I've got only two more problems to do, but the trouble is, I can't do either of them."

Reddy, the Beldens' mischievous Irish setter, lay sleeping on the braided rug at Trixie's feet. Trixie nudged him gently with the toe of her sneaker.

"It's all right for you," she told him gloomily. "You don't have to worry about anything."

Reddy didn't even bother to open his eyes. He

thumped his tail once, just to let her know he'd heard, and immediately went back to sleep.

Impatient, Trixie sighed and ran one hand through her unruly curls. "What's taking Brian and Mart so long, anyway?" she asked Honey, who merely smiled in sympathy and bent again to her work.

For a while, there was silence in the warm, fragrant kitchen of the old farmhouse. As always, it looked cozy in the lamplight. Its walls were hung with gleaming copper utensils. Treasured china was proudly displayed on plate racks and cup hooks.

Trixie gazed toward the kitchen door, hoping to see her two older brothers. Half an hour before, they had promised to be "back in a flash" from putting the youngest Belden, six-year-old Bobby, to bed. Judging from the muffled sounds of hilarity coming from upstairs, however, Trixie guessed that all three of her brothers had forgotten about her.

Normally it would have been Trixie's job to put Bobby to bed whenever her parents were out for an evening, visiting friends. This was not one of the chores Trixie disliked. Looking after Bobby was usually a pleasure—unless she also had math homework to do.

On this Friday evening in November, Trixie

knew that Brian and Mart were trying to help her. All the same, she couldn't help wishing that their help also included explaining all the puzzling problems she'd had to wrestle with all evening.

Honey smiled at a particularly loud thump that came from upstairs. "It sounds as if they're having fun," she remarked. "Maybe they're having a pillow fight." Her hazel eyes twinkled.

Trixie frowned. "If so, Bobby will be so excited, he'll never get to sleep. Ooh, that Mart! He ought to know better. As for Brian, I'm surprised he didn't put a stop to it long ago."

Honey couldn't help agreeing. She knew, as did everyone else, that seventeen-year-old Brian was the most level-headed and even-tempered of the Belden children.

Fifteen-year-old Mart, on the other hand, loved to entertain anyone who would listen to him. He used big words to confound his audiences—and, in particular, to tease Trixie. Just eleven months older than his sister, Mart was Trixie's "almost-twin."

Honey laid down her pencil at last. "There!" she said with satisfaction. "I'm all through for the evening. Would you like me to go up and get Bobby into bed?"

"That would be terrific," Trixie said gratefully. "And while you're at it, tell Brian and Mart that I need their help in the kitchen."

"I'll do my best," her friend promised. "After all, if I'm spending the night, you could say it's to my advantage to see that Bobby gets off to sleep pronto!"

Trixie smiled as Honey left the room. She thought, as she had so many times before, how glad she was that her friend felt almost as much at home at Crabapple Farm as she herself did.

The Beldens enjoyed a quiet but comfortable life at the old farmhouse, situated near the east bank of the beautiful Hudson River in New York.

Honey lived in nearby Manor House. It was a more luxurious and stately home than Trixie's, with grounds that included a stable filled with horses, a lake for swimming and boating in the summer, and a game preserve that covered many acres.

Trixie and Honey, both fourteen years old, had been friends from the first moment they'd met. Honey was taller and slimmer than Trixie. Her real name was Madeleine, though no one had called her that for a very long time. Her nickname had come about because of her lovely shoulder-length golden hair and her sweet disposition.

Almost at once, the two girls had become involved in many exciting adventures and puzzling mysteries.

While Trixie and Honey were solving their first two mysteries, they had also rescued red-haired Jim Frayne from the clutches of his cruel stepfather.

Soon afterward, Honey's parents had adopted Jim. Now Jim, Trixie, Honey, Brian, and Mart belonged to a semisecret club, together with Diana Lynch, who lived on a magnificent estate nearby, and Dan Mangan, nephew of Regan, the Wheelers' groom. They called themselves the Bob-Whites of the Glen.

Tonight, however, Trixie wasn't even thinking about the Bob-Whites, or even about the detective agency she and Honey hoped to open one day. She was too intent on trying to solve the riddle of her last math problem.

"Listen to this, Reddy," she said, nudging the Irish setter once more. She picked up her math book and read aloud, " 'Take two apples from three apples and what do you have?' "

Reddy's eyes popped open, and he raised his head.

"Well, come on," Trixie said impatiently. "What's the answer? I'll bet you think this is an easy one, right? I'll bet you're thinking to yourself, *Take two apples from three apples, and you have one apple.*"

Reddy gathered his legs under him and lurched to his feet.

"But that's the answer I gave in class today," Trixie continued, "and it's wrong. Do you hear me, you dumb dog? It's wrong!"

Reddy growled deep in his throat. Then, to her astonishment, he barked loud and long.

For a moment, Trixie thought that Reddy had understood every word she'd said—particularly her statement concerning his intelligence, which she hadn't meant. A second later, though, she understood the family pet's agitation. Someone was pounding urgently on the front door.

Just before she hurried to see who could be calling on them at nine o'clock at night, Trixie flung over her shoulder at Reddy, "Whoever it is, I hope they're better at math than you are."

Reddy, apparently deciding that he'd done his canine duty for the time being, merely tried to look wise, smug, and reproachful all at once and promptly collapsed again onto the kitchen floor. He had gone back to sleep before Trixie even left the room.

Reddy's barking had also summoned Brian, Mart, and Honey. As Trixie reached the front door, the three were hurrying down the stairs.

"Who is it?" Brian called.

"Methinks our sibling is not gifted with X-ray vision," Mart said loftily from behind him. "Let her open yon portal first. Then, mayhap, she can

19

respond to your interrogation."

Trixie grinned as she opened 'yon portal,' but her grin faded as she found herself staring at the slight, disheveled figure of one of her classmates, Fay Franklin. Fay was new in the neighborhood, having moved to Sleepyside-on-the-Hudson with her mother only a few weeks before.

There was no doubt that Fay was upset. Her winter jacket looked as if it had been thrown hastily around her slim shoulders. Her short, dark curls were tumbled about her pretty face, which, at the moment, seemed pale with shock.

"Why, Fay!" Trixie exclaimed in surprise. "What is it? Is something wrong?"

It was soon obvious that Fay was too breathless to do anything more than lean against the door-jamb and gaze at the circle of concerned young faces around her.

Willing hands reached toward her and drew her into the warm, cozy living room.

Fay struggled to catch her breath. "Oh, please," she gasped at last. "I—I'm sorry to burst in on you all like this, but I need your help. It—it's my mother. She's had an accident, and our phone is out of order."

Brian's gaze sharpened at once. As always, he was instantly concerned when he heard of anyone being sick or injured. He intended to become a doctor, and everyone who knew him was certain he would make a very fine one.

"Accident?" he echoed now. "What kind of accident? Is she badly hurt?"

Fay gulped. "It—it's her hip," she explained. "I—that is, we—think it's broken."

Trixie listened closely as Fay told them that her mother worked as a housekeeper for one of the local residents. Fay was still unsure exactly what had happened. But something, she thought, had startled Mrs. Franklin as she was reaching into a kitchen cupboard.

"And she slipped and fell," Fay finished, catching her breath on a sob, "and now she can't move. I've had to leave her alone to come and get help. . . ."

Brian didn't need to hear any more. "Don't worry. I'll see to this. I'll get in touch with Dr. Ferris at once, and then I'll drive you home. We can wait for him there. Once he hears about this, he'll probably send for an ambulance. Where did you say you lived?"

"Lisgard House," Fay answered.

Mart's jaw dropped. "Lisgard House? But that's the place—I mean, isn't it haunt—?" He stopped abruptly as Trixie dug him in the ribs with her elbow.

Fay didn't appear to have heard Mart's remark. She was still watching Brian as he strode quickly across the room toward the telephone.

"Trix, Mart," Brian ordered over his shoulder, "you'd better plan on coming with us to Fay's house. We may need all the help we can get." Soon he was engaged in a low-voiced conversation with someone on the other end of the line.

"I'll come, too," Honey announced suddenly. "Maybe there's some way I can help, too."

"How 'bout me?" a forlorn young voice asked from the stairs. "Can I come?"

"Wow!" Trixie breathed. "We forgot all about Bobby!" She hurried toward the small pajama-clad figure. "You should have been asleep ages ago, you rascal," she told him.

Bobby grinned up at her. "Mart gave me a bath with lots and lots of bubbles," he announced. "There were so many bubbles that it took Brian ages and ages to clean them up. Then Mart told me a scary story about a mean ol' witch who used to live in a big ol' house around here."

Mart shuffled his feet and looked uncomfortable. "Uh—I—er—this is kind of a coincidence," he mumbled. "I didn't know Fay would be arriving, and I—er—that is, I guess I got carried away. And then when Honey came up, she wanted to find out how the story ended. . . ."

All at once, Trixie realized which witch story Mart must have told. She smothered a gasp and

22

said hastily, "You can tell me about it tomorrow, Bobby. Right now it's time for bed."

But Bobby wasn't about to leave. "Mart said the witch lived in Sleepyside a long, long time ago, and she did bad things to people. She looked at their crops and stuff, like this." He scowled ferociously. "And you know what else she did?"

"I already know," Trixie replied, trying unsuccessfully to urge him back up the stairs.

Bobby stood his ground. "First you have to guess what she did next."

Fay moved toward him. "Why don't you tell me what she did next, Bobby?" she said gently.

Mart looked more uncomfortable than ever. He thrust his hands deep into the pockets of his jeans. "Listen, Fay, it's just a dumb story," he mumbled. "Anyway, you must have heard it all before."

Fay nodded slowly. "I've heard some of it, of course," she said, "but never quite this way. Come on, Bobby. What happened next?"

Trixie watched helplessly as Bobby promptly plopped down on a step and peeked at them through a banister railing. "So the mean ol' witch made the crops die. And she made people sick, like this." He clutched at his throat, rolled his eyes, and gurgled horribly in the back of his throat.

In spite of herself, Honey giggled. Then, almost immediately, she looked sheepishly at Trixie. "I know we shouldn't have excited Bobby," she said, "but when I arrived upstairs, Mart was just getting to the most exciting part—"

"And Honey never heard this story before," Bobby told Trixie proudly, " 'cause she didn't live here when she was a little girl. So Mart told Honey all about the witch's piece of 'sistance."

"That's *piéce de résistance*," Mart corrected him, unable to resist it.

Fay smiled. "And what was the 'piece of 'sistance'?"

"The mean ol' witch chased bad little boys who wouldn't go to sleep," Bobby stated, a note of awe in his voice. "And when she caught them, she wiggled her fingers at them and said—and said—What did she say, Mart?"

"I've forgotten," Mart replied, still avoiding Trixie's eyes.

"But I'd like to hear it," Fay said gently.

"Me, too," snapped Trixie.

Mart sighed. "The witch wiggled her fingers and said: 'Abracadabra and hair of a dog. Bat's wings and spiders. Heh-heh! You're a frog!' "

Trixie moaned and glared at him.

"And she turned all the little boys into green frogs," Bobby said. "They had to go hopping off into Martin's Marsh forever. And today you can still hear them going *ribbit, ribbit, ribbit!*"

"Okay, short stuff," Mart said, moving toward him. "That's the end, so let's go back to bed, okay?"

"But that's not the end," Bobby protested. "The people of Sleepyside didn't like their crops and stuff turning brown. They didn't like getting sick. And they didn't like their little boys getting turned into frogs. So one night, you know what they did? They set fire to the witch's house—with her in it! She was barbecued, Trix!" Bobby's voice was triumphant.

"Oh, Mart!" Trixie said. "How could you tell him a story like that at bedtime?"

"I liked it," Bobby told her, "and I liked the last part, too, 'cause you know what happened next? Someone built a new house where the burned-down one was. And the witch's ghost still lives there! Mart says the witch goes moaning through all the rooms, like this: 'Whooo! Whooooooo! Whooo—' "

He broke off suddenly as he caught sight of Trixie's determined face. "I think I'd better go to bed," he finished hastily.

"I think I'll come with you," Mart said. "I'll tell you what, shrimp. I'll tuck you in and stay while the others are leaving."

Undaunted, Bobby looked up at him and asked, "Will you tell me another story?"

Mart didn't look at Trixie. "I'll tell you the story

25

of Peter Rabbit," he answered, "or maybe the one about the tiger who looked like a pussycat. But something tells me I'd better not tell you another ghost story, okay?" Bobby's bedroom door closed firmly behind them.

Trixie glanced quickly at Fay. "I'm sorry," she said. "Mart would never have told that story if he'd known you were going to be here."

"It's okay, really," Fay answered. "It's interesting to hear someone else's version of what happened." She turned and hurried toward Brian, who had just hung up the telephone receiver. "Did you get hold of the doctor, Brian? Is he coming right away?"

Brian smiled at her reassuringly. "Everything's all set," he answered, reaching for his car keys. "Let's go."

Honey shrugged herself into her jacket. "Trix, why did you tell Fay you were sorry?" she whispered. "What's the big deal about telling her the witch story?"

Trixie paused at the front door. "Oh, Honey, didn't you know?" she asked softly. "The old mansion Bobby was talking about was Lisgard House. The house is supposed to be haunted, just the way he said."

Honey still looked puzzled. "So?"

"So Fay and her mother moved into it just a few

weeks ago," Trixie answered. "Hold on to your hat, Honey. We're about to visit a ghost!"

Moments later, Trixie's feelings were mixed as Brian's old jalopy sped along Glen Road. She was, of course, very sorry that Fay's mother had been hurt. On the other hand, she couldn't help feeling a tingle of excitement as she thought of the mysterious nineteenth-century mansion they were about to see.

Lisgard House had fascinated Trixie for as long as she could remember. Situated close to Martin's Marsh, it was surrounded by iron railings and locked gates. Every weekday, in the bus, when Trixie passed it on her way to and from Sleepyside Junior-Senior High School, she could never resist craning her neck to see over the thick growth of foliage that almost hid the place from view.

Although Mart had exaggerated in telling the story to Bobby, it was true that, at one time, a witch *was* supposed to have lived in the old mansion. The original house, with the witch inside it, *had* been burned. And the mansion that had been rebuilt on the site *was* supposed to be haunted by Sarah Sligo's ghost.

Trixie had often hoped to catch a glimpse of the ghostly figure said to haunt the house, but to her intense disappointment, she never had.

Over the years, none of the Lisgards had encouraged visitors. The last Lisgard of them all, old Caleb, had been the worst of them. A mean-spirited and short-tempered man, he had been a recluse. For the last years of his life, he had shut himself away from the world and had refused to see anyone, except for the odd servant or two whom he had managed, with difficulty, to hire.

He had died only a few months before. Trixie knew that the house had been inherited by a nephew-in-law, Lewis Gregory. She wondered what he was like. Most of all, she wondered what on earth had persuaded Fay and her mother to come to work in such a gloomy place.

Brian pulled up beside the enormous iron front gates that faced Glen Road.

"Oh, no, Brian," Fay said hurriedly, "we won't go in this way. Take this side turn here. It leads to the back of the house. I—I left the gates there unlocked purposely so I could get back in quickly."

Honey shivered as Brian's car turned away from the familiarity of the lighted road and bumped its way along a rutted lane that ran alongside tall, spiked railings. High trees, growing on either side of the potholed road, stretched bare arms to the black sky, and birds, disturbed by the noise of the car's engine, flew, in alarm from the branches.

"We're almost there," Fay announced breathlessly, leaning forward across Brian's shoulder. "Here! Turn here!"

Obediently, Brian twisted the wheel and drove through iron gates, smaller than the massive ones in front, though somehow just as forbidding.

Trixie knew that Martin's Marsh lay close behind them. She felt Honey clutch her arm.

"Listen, Trix," Honey commanded. "Can you hear them?"

As Brian pulled up beside the door that was obviously intended to be the service entrance, he turned off the car's engine. It was then that Trixie heard the sounds that had caught Honey's attention.

Ribbit, ribbit, ribbit!

Trixie laughed. "It's only the marsh frogs," she said.

"Or little boys who've been enchanted by the witch's spell," Honey answered, still trembling.

Brian and Fay had already jumped from the car and hurried into the house.

Trixie and Honey were about to follow them, when, all at once, Trixie stiffened. Her gaze focused on something over Honey's shoulder.

Her friend cried out in alarm at the expression on Trixie's intent face. "Trixie! What is it? What's the matter? What do you see?"

Trixie stared at the dim outline of a figure that had suddenly appeared around the corner of the house. It seemed to hesitate for one long moment. Then, as Trixie watched, it faded silently into the dark shadows behind it.

Trixie gasped and could almost hear the pounding of her own heart. "Oh, Honey," she said at last, "I'm not sure—but I think I've just seen the witch's ghost!"

Trixie Is Warned · 2

HONEY STARED and turned her head quickly toward the dark shadows. "G-Ghost?" she quavered. "Are you sure it was the ghost?"

Trixie frowned. "No," she said slowly, "I'm not sure at all. It came and it went, almost before I realized it." She told Honey exactly what she'd seen.

Honey's teeth chattered. "Whatever it was, I don't like the sound of it, Trix. Do you suppose the others would miss us if we went home?"

Trixie couldn't blame her friend for feeling nervous. She almost felt the same way herself— almost, but not quite. It would be unthinkable to pass up this terrific opportunity to see the inside of a genuine haunted house, after all the years of wanting to.

All the same, it took all of Trixie's powers of persuasion to get Honey to follow her inside. It was only when Trixie reminded her friend about their errand of mercy that Honey agreed, at last, to follow her.

Once inside the back door, Honey almost turned right around and walked out again.

The two girls found themselves standing in a long, dimly lit passageway. Its dark-paneled walls were gloomy and forbidding. Trixie later discovered that the walls throughout the house were paneled with this same dark, somber wood, barely relieved by a dismal-looking picture here and there.

"I don't believe this place," Honey breathed, gazing about her. "Whoever decorated the hallway certainly had taste—all of it bad!"

Trixie grinned in agreement and followed the sound of voices coming from an open doorway.

She could hear Brian's deep tones and Fay's lighter ones—and one other voice, which, she correctly guessed, was that of Fay's mother.

Trixie spared only one glance for the gloomy kitchen, shuddered as she noticed the dark green paint, and hurried at once to her brother's side.

Brian was crouched beside a middle-aged woman who lay awkwardly on the floor. Her head was cradled by a pillow pulled hastily, Trixie assumed, from someone's bed. Her features, which in normal circumstances would have resembled her daughter's, were twisted with pain.

"Now, stay still and try not to worry," Brian was saying. "Both the doctor and the ambulance will be here soon." He looked up. "You know, Trix, it might not be a bad idea if someone went and stood at that front gate to let them in."

"I'll go," Fay said at once. "I'll have to direct them around to the back. They can't get in the front way. Those gates are locked, and I don't have the key."

"Then who's got it?" Trixie asked.

Fay hesitated. "Our odd-job man, Zeke. He—he's not here right now. . . ." She hurried from the room.

Brian introduced both Trixie and Honey to Mrs. Franklin, who said, "I'm sorry to be such a nuisance. I can't think how this could have happened—"

It was strange, but Trixie thought she could detect a note of reserve in Mrs. Franklin's voice. It was almost as if she knew something that she wasn't about to tell anyone.

"Try not to worry about it," Brian repeated.

33

Mrs. Franklin tried to smile. "I'm trying not to," she said, "but I can't help worrying about— about everything. It's so silly that this had to happen, what with Mr. Gregory being away and everything. He's not due back from his business trip till tomorrow afternoon, you see." She looked anxiously at Brian. "I suppose I *will* have to go to the hospital."

Brian nodded his dark head. "Yes, and I think you'd better plan on being there for a few days, Mrs. Franklin," he said.

Suddenly Trixie realized one of the things that must be worrying the injured woman. She bent down and said gently, "Please don't trouble yourself about what's going to happen to Fay while you're gone. She can stay with us at Crabapple Farm for as long as she wants. Moms won't mind at all. In fact, if she were here, she would be the first one to think of it."

"That's right," Brian confirmed quickly. "It was dumb of me not to have suggested it myself."

"She can come and stay with me, too," Honey put in eagerly. "We have lots of room in our house, and anything would be better than having to stay here—" She broke off, suddenly realizing what she'd said.

Mrs. Franklin laughed. "Please don't look so guilty, dear," she said. "I do know what you mean. But it's not so bad working here, really. Sometimes, when the sun's shining, the old house looks almost cheerful."

Trixie glanced at the gloomy kitchen and thought again of the long shadows in the passage outside. She wondered if the rest of the house was any better. If it was worse, she couldn't imagine that anything about the old mansion could ever look cheerful.

Mrs. Franklin seemed to sense Trixie's thoughts. "We—Fay and I—haven't been here long, as you know," she explained. "We were living in New York City until recently, but I needed a job badly. I'm a widow, you see, and it isn't easy—" She paused. "Then I came across Mr. Gregory's ad for a housekeeper. I—I jumped at the chance at once. The wages are good—very good."

They'd have to be, Trixie thought, *if Mr. Gregory wanted to keep any servant working here. I wonder how much Mrs. Franklin knows about the history of this place?*

"I think someone's arriving at last!" Brian exclaimed, jumping to his feet.

He was right. Trixie heard the back door slam, and soon brisk footsteps sounded in the passage.

"All right," a cheerful voice said. "Now, what's going on here?" It was Dr. Ferris.

After that, everything seemed to happen at

once. It wasn't any time at all before the ambulance, too, had arrived. The white-coated attendants looked, Trixie thought, a little nervous and apprehensive. Under Dr. Ferris's supervision, they transferred Mrs. Franklin from floor to stretcher, while Fay hovered anxiously behind them.

"All right, boys, easy now," Dr. Ferris ordered as, with the stretcher, they made their way carefully to the kitchen door. "You get along to the hospital as quickly as you can. I'll meet you there."

"Whew!" Trixie heard one of the attendants say as they left the room. "I'll sure be glad to get out of this place. It gives me the creeps. How about you, Harry?"

Trixie was never to learn what Harry's reaction was, for Dr. Ferris was already giving Fay brisk instructions.

"No, young lady," he was telling her, "you don't need to come with me. There's nothing you can do tonight, and you'll only be in the way. It's a broken hip all right, and the next item on the agenda is to set it. Take my word for it, your mother is going to be just fine. She won't feel a thing. We'll put her to sleep to do this job, and she'll snooze like a baby when we're through. You just concentrate on looking after yourself. If I need you, I know where to find you. Don't worry about a thing. You going to stay here?"

Trixie took a step forward. "Fay's coming with us to Crabapple Farm," she said. "At least, she can if she wants to. Honey's invited her to Manor House, too."

Fay smiled faintly but shook her curly head. "Thank you—all of you—but I think I'd better stay here."

Honey shivered and glanced around her. "Stay here? Oh, Fay, why would anyone want to stay in this spooky place—?" She broke off, realizing that she'd been guilty of tactlessness again.

"I know Mr. Gregory—my mother's employer —wouldn't want the house left empty," Fay explained, "and now there's no one but me to look after it. There're a lot of valuable antiques here, you see."

Dr. Ferris reached for his bag. "Ah, well, I'll let you youngsters argue this out among yourselves." He turned and strode toward the door. "In the meantime, young lady," he said to Fay, "I'll leave word at the hospital that you can visit your mother tomorrow morning—not before, understand?"

He waved a cheerful hand and was gone. A moment later, they heard the sound of his car's engine as it followed the wailing ambulance out of the grounds.

"Don't worry," Brian told Fay. "Your mother

37

will be fine. We've known Dr. Ferris for years, and he's the best there is."

Trixie set her jaw. "Now, about staying here alone tonight—"

Fay turned away from the door where she'd been standing. "It's very kind of you," she said, "but I've made up my mind. This job means a lot to my mother and me, and we—we don't want to lose it. I appreciate your offer, honestly, but I'd better stay."

There was silence. Trixie knew only too well what she had to do next, and she could tell that Honey did, too. Honey was already looking as nervous and as apprehensive as those ambulance attendants had.

Trixie took a deep breath. "Honey and I feel that you shouldn't stay here alone," she said at last. "So we'll be glad to stay here with you—if you'd like us to, that is."

Fay jumped at their offer with such alacrity that Trixie realized that their new friend really hadn't wanted to stay alone, any more than they themselves would have wanted to.

"Then that's settled," Trixie said, glancing at Honey out of the corner of her eye.

"Of course," Honey said faintly. "I know my parents won't mind. They think I'm spending the night at Trixie's, anyway."

"I really appreciate this." Fay sounded grateful. "I'd better see to the sleeping arrangements. My mother and I usually share a small room over there—off the kitchen. It does have twin beds, and there's also a very comfortable armchair. I could make that up for one of us." She hurried away.

Brian picked up the pillow from the floor and placed it, unthinkingly, on a kitchen counter. "Are you two sure you're going to be okay?" he asked, his forehead wrinkled.

"Of course we'll be okay," Trixie answered, sounding more sure than she felt. "Why wouldn't we be?"

Honey moved toward the door. "I'd better go and help Fay," she said nervously. "If I stand here doing nothing, I'm going to change my mind and come home with you, Brian. Jeepers! Imagine spending a night in a haunted house voluntarily. I must be crazy!"

Trixie didn't say anything until Honey had left the room. Then she told Brian, "You'll have to explain to Moms and Dad what's happened. Maybe you'd better phone Manor House and tell them, too. Okay, Brian?"

"Sure." Her brother turned toward the door, then hesitated. "Listen, Trix, you're not worried about staying in this place tonight, are you? A lot of the tales told about Lisgard House, if not most

39

of them, are just local gossip, you know."

"I know," Trixie answered slowly, "but I can't help wondering how much of it is true."

"I'm sure some of it is," Brian said. "But you have to remember that stories passed by word of mouth for generations tend to get bent out of shape over the years. You heard Mart's version tonight, for example."

Trixie frowned. "What about seeing the witch's ghost?" she asked, thinking of the dim figure she'd seen such a short time before. She told Brian about it.

He laughed. "It was probably only old Zeke Collins, Trix. He's the odd-job man around here, as you know."

Trixie was puzzled. "But if it was Zeke, why wouldn't he have come to help? He must have known something was going on—especially when he noticed the doctor's car, to say nothing of the ambulance."

Brian shrugged his shoulders. "He's supposed to be one of those characters who keep to themselves, Trix. Maybe he thought it was none of his business and just turned around and went home. He lives somewhere on these grounds. He's got a cottage here, I think."

Trixie wasn't sure whether she was pleased or sorry to hear this sensible explanation. Too, she wasn't sure she believed it. The figure she'd seen could have been that of Zeke Collins, she supposed. But what if it hadn't been? Could it have been the witch's ghost? More important, did she really believe in ghosts, anyway? Sometimes she was certain that she didn't believe at all that a person could return in any way, shape, or form after death.

On the other hand, she thought, *sometimes strange things happen—and there doesn't seem to be any logical explanation for them.*

After Brian had gone, Trixie stood alone in the gloomy kitchen and listened to the sound of his old jalopy as it faded away in the distance.

"Maybe I shouldn't have been so quick to offer to stay here with Fay tonight," she muttered to herself. "Maybe we should have insisted that she come home with us, instead." She sighed. "Oh, well! I've really done it this time." She looked up at the dark ceiling, as if some spirit hovering there could hear her. "Listen, Miss Witch," she spoke up. "Are you there? If you're going to do any haunting tonight, do me a favor and wait till I'm asleep, okay?"

There was a sudden silence, as if the whole house were holding its breath.

Then someone whispered, *"Beware!"*

Touring a Haunted House · 3

TRIXIE GASPED. "What? What did you say?" She spun around to look behind her and saw Honey hurrying into the kitchen.

"Everything's all set," Honey announced, sounding pleased, "and guess what, Trix? I was telling Fay about your 'ghost,' and she says it was probably only old Zeke Collins. He lives on the grounds, you know. Fay says he often snoops around. This time she thought he was off somewhere in town, but he must have been here all along. Aren't you glad?"

Trixie wasn't listening. "Honey, did you—that is—before you said what you just said, did you say something else? Did you say anything at all?"

Honey looked surprised. "Of course I said something else. I said lots of something elses. I told Fay we'd toss for which one of us is going to sleep in the armchair. Fay offered to sleep in it herself, Trix, but it doesn't look too comfortable, so I think my way is more fair. Then I told her we were glad she'd come to Sleepyside. I still don't understand how anyone could willingly live in a house like this. But I didn't say that this time, Trixie. . . ."

Trixie watched as her friend chattered on. At first she thought that Honey seemed more relaxed and less apprehensive than she'd been when they'd first arrived at the house. Then she realized that Honey was still nervous about spending the night there. Knowing that Fay needed company tonight, though, had made her bravely decide to cover up her fears.

Trixie also realized that, whoever it was who had warned her to beware, it certainly hadn't been Honey. Had it been anyone at all? Or had Trixie's ears been playing tricks on her? Mart had told her often enough that she had an overactive imagination.

Trixie decided not to tell Honey anything about the strange whisper—not just yet, anyway.

Honey was still talking when Fay appeared in

the doorway. "Our room's all ready, Trixie," Fay announced, "so we can turn in whenever we like. You know, it's very kind of both of you, staying here like this. . . ."

Trixie and Honey both moved to her sides and took hold of her arms.

"We're only too glad to help out a neighbor," Trixie said awkwardly. She always felt uncomfortable when she was thanked for being kind.

"Are you hungry?" Fay asked shyly, looking from one to the other. "Would you like a snack before we turn in? I make a great cup of hot chocolate."

"Hot chocolate would be nice about now," Honey admitted. "What do you think, Trix?"

But Trixie's thoughts were far from the delights of hot chocolate. She was remembering the strange voice she'd just heard. She thought about the mysterious figure she'd seen outside, who might or might not have been Zeke Collins.

"Fay, is there anyone else in the house—besides us, I mean?" she asked suddenly.

Trixie heard Fay catch her breath sharply. "Someone else? Why, no. There's no one."

Fay had answered quickly—almost too quickly, as if she were trying to convince herself as much as her friends.

"In that case," Trixie said, still watching Fay

closely, "could we—that is, would you mind, I mean—could we look over the house? I've always wanted to, and this seems such a terrific chance."

And if I'm going to sleep here, Trixie thought to herself, *I'd like to make sure that all the doors and windows are locked up tight.*

For one brief moment, Fay seemed to hesitate. Then she said, "Why, of course, Trixie. I'd have offered to show you around before this, but there's really not that much to see. Old Mr. Lisgard kept a lot of the rooms shut up. That way, he figured they didn't have to be cleaned very often."

"Or even at all," Trixie added, remembering the stories that had been told in Sleepyside. Mr. Caleb Lisgard had been a skinflint. It was said that he begrudged every penny he'd ever had to spend.

Fay smiled and led the way toward the front of the house, flipping on light switches as she went.

Honey pressed close to Trixie's side. "I don't like this," she muttered. "What was wrong with drinking our hot chocolate and then just going to bed? Supposing we meet up with that ghost Mart was talking about?"

Trixie had been wondering the same thing, but she thought it might be best not to mention it. "Remember," she whispered, "the Lisgard family lived here for generations, and they didn't seem to

45

be bothered by any old ghost.''

"And there's one thing *you* should remember, Trix,'' Honey retorted. "There aren't any Lisgards left to tell us anything different. They're all dead, aren't they?''

Trixie chuckled and hurried to join Fay at what was obviously the old mansion's front entrance hall.

Trixie glanced quickly at the large front doors and noticed at once that they were bolted at both top and bottom. She sighed with relief.

She turned her attention to the dingy, dark-paneled walls and made a face when she saw the stuffed animal heads that hung there.

Fay looked apologetic, almost as though it was her fault that some long-ago Lisgard had been a big-game hunter. "Pretty awful, aren't they?'' she said softly. "We—my mother and I—wish that Mr. Gregory would take them down. It makes me want to cry when I think that these poor creatures had to die just to provide a trophy for someone's walls.''

Trixie agreed wholeheartedly. She was about to say so when she noticed that Honey's attention had been caught by a striking picture, one of the few hanging in the hallway. Simply framed, it was an oil painting of a clown dressed in a blue costume.

"Why, Fay!" Honey exclaimed. "Isn't this a Picasso? If so, it looks like the real thing!"

"It *is* the real thing," Fay confirmed, smiling. "If you'll look closer, you'll see the signature. That picture is just about the only thing Mr. Gregory brought with him when he moved in here. He's very proud of it because he says he bought it from someone who didn't realize its true value. It's worth a lot of money now." She sighed. "A lot of things in this house are worth a lot of money. Most of the furniture has been here for such a long time that the pieces have become antiques. But I guess that picture is about the only thing in the house I really like. You'll see what I mean in a minute."

It wasn't long before Trixie and Honey did indeed see what Fay meant. Their new friend led them through downstairs rooms filled with heavy, old-fashioned furniture. Even though Fay flipped on light switches, nothing could dispel the ever-present gloom of the place.

Some of the furniture was covered with dust sheets. Whatever wasn't, Trixie thought, should have been. She couldn't help comparing the contents of this house with the contents of the Beldens' cozy farmhouse. She didn't have to think twice about which she preferred!

By the time most of the downstairs rooms had

been thoroughly explored, Honey seemed, if not completely relaxed, then at least less nervous than she had been when they'd first arrived.

They were standing in the middle of the large living room when she told Trixie in a low voice, "We've been in old houses before, and this one doesn't seem so very different to me. I know you don't like the furniture—" she glanced toward an ornately carved coffee table that stood in front of the big, empty fireplace—"but it *is* very valuable; take my word for it. I wonder if it's insured."

When she was asked, Fay nodded her dark head. "Yes, it's all insured," she answered. "Once old Mr. Lisgard found out how much his furniture was worth, he made sure that if anything ever happened to it, someone would have to pay him to replace it."

"And that someone was the insurance company?" Trixie asked.

"Yes."

Fay turned and began to lead the way toward the front hall again, but Trixie put out a hand to stop her.

"Isn't that another room over there?" she asked, nodding toward a door that was almost hidden by a tall bookcase.

Fay hesitated for a moment. "It's only old Mr. Lisgard's study," she replied at last. "It—it hasn't been used since he died. You can see it, if you really want to."

Ignoring the odd note in Fay's voice, Trixie moved toward the room at once and, in another second, was standing inside it.

She could sense immediately that there was something about it that was different from the rest. It was small, and as dark and as gloomy as all the others. It held the usual conglomeration of period furniture, none of it matching. She noticed the antique desk that stood against the room's only window and assumed that this was where Caleb Lisgard had done his work.

But it was neither the gloom nor the furniture that made this room strangely forbidding. It was something in the very air of the place—something cold, unwelcoming, and oddly hostile.

Trixie shivered. "I don't know how any Lisgard, man or woman, could like this room," she remarked. She turned her head and noticed that only Honey had followed her through the door. Fay still stood where they had left her, in the living room.

Fay moved closer to her friends, but Trixie noticed that she still did not step across the threshold. "I know you'll think I'm being silly," Fay said, "but I don't like going into that room."

Suddenly Trixie understood. "Wasn't this the one where the witch—her name was Sarah Sligo,

49

by the way—was burned to death?"

Fay moved restlessly. "Yes—at least, that's what I've heard. The original room, of course, was burned down, along with the rest of the house. But someone else, a wealthy merchant, I think, rebuilt the mansion exactly the way it had been. And he rebuilt that room along with it."

"I'm sure I don't blame you for not liking it," Honey remarked loyally. "The study is enough to give anyone the creeps. This old desk is nice, though. It's a Governor Winthrop, I think." She touched it lightly with a reverent fingertip.

A half an hour later, the three girls were back in Fay's bedroom, the tour complete. There had been no new surprises—no more rooms to frighten anyone. Trixie had seen enough old furniture to last her a lifetime, while Honey repeated, though not in Fay's hearing, that she couldn't understand how anyone could live in such a mausoleum. More important, Trixie had made sure that all doors and windows to the outside were securely locked. She also still had no clue to the source of the mysterious voice she had heard.

It wasn't long before Fay had made them the promised hot chocolate, and soon afterward, Trixie climbed into a pair of borrowed pajamas, tossed a coin, lost the call, and found herself scrambling between the thick, fluffy blankets waiting for her on the bedroom's only armchair.

Trixie watched as Honey made herself comfortable in what was, she assumed, normally Mrs. Franklin's bed.

Behind it was a photograph of a man and a woman holding a chubby, dark-haired baby.

Fay followed Trixie's glance and smiled shyly. "That's my parents—and me. My father died when I was very young—not much older than I was there. Mother and I are very close, and she's always worked very hard to give me the things I need. Right now, we're saving for the time when I go to college."

Trixie and Honey exchanged glances. They knew now why Mrs. Franklin and her daughter stayed at Lisgard House, in spite of its reputation. They needed the money.

For the first time, Trixie had a chance to take note of this small room. Someone, probably Mrs. Franklin, had done the best she could to make it as cozy as the circumstances would allow.

Next door to the kitchen, the room had no window of its own. Its only door opened onto that same dark passage that led from the back entrance. Its walls, though, had been hung with bright travel posters and photographs of long-ago movie stars.

Trixie thought of the back door and wondered if

it, too, was locked and bolted. *I must remember to check on that when the others are asleep*, she thought.

Fay was about to scramble into her own bed when she said suddenly, "Trixie, what *is* the real story about the witch—what was her name, Sarah Sligo? I've heard so many tales since we moved in here. It's hard to try and figure out which one to believe."

"Yes, Trix," Honey said, leaning up on one elbow, "tell us what really happened. I'd like to hear the story again, too."

Fay frowned. "I thought you were learning about the witch for the first time tonight, Honey. At least, that's what Bobby said."

Trixie laughed. "Honey's just got a kind heart," she declared. "Both Mart and Bobby were having such a good time that she didn't want to tell them she'd heard the legend many times before. Remember, Fay, we pass this house every day on our way to school, so of course I told her about it."

Fay climbed between the covers and propped her pillow behind her back. "I'm ready," she said breathlessly.

"Me, too," Honey declared, smiling across the room at Trixie.

Trixie hesitated, frowning. Around her the house was silent. All at once, she had the same weird feeling that she'd had before. It was almost as if someone—or something—were holding its breath and waiting to hear what she was going to say.

Then, as she still hesitated, she had a sudden hunch that she didn't like at all. She felt that she was about to make a terrible mistake.

The Witch's Curse · 4

TRIXIE BIT HER LIP and looked down at her hands. "Why—why don't we leave it for tonight?" she said at last. "I'll tell you tomorrow. In any case, there isn't much left to tell." She began to slide under the covers.

Honey's voice stopped her. "Jeepers, Trix!" she exclaimed. "Since when did you pass up a chance to tell a story to an eager audience—in this case, us?" She grinned and waved a hand at the other bed.

"Yes, Trixie. Please tell us." Fay's voice was oddly urgent. "Besides, I—I don't think I feel very sleepy just yet. I can't help wondering what's going on at the hospital with my mother."

"Forget it, Fay," Honey told her firmly. "You know what Dr. Ferris said. Your mother will be fine. Really. Come on, Trix! Story, please! We need something to get Fay's mind off her troubles."

"Well, it's hard to know where to start," Trixie answered uncertainly.

"There was once a young woman named Sarah Sligo," Honey prompted her. "She lived in this house many, many years ago. Some people thought she was weird, because she wore a tall, black hat and one of those billowy black cloaks that reach almost to the ground."

Fay looked puzzled. "You mean people thought she was a witch just because of her clothes?"

Trixie shook her head. "It wasn't only her clothes. It was lots of other things, too. You see, she used to spend a great deal of time wandering around Martin's Marsh. It seemed that she picked flowers and herbs and stuff like that. My dad thinks that maybe she used them to mix up healing medicines. He thinks she was a sort of unofficial doctor to the town and tried to help both sick people and sick animals get well again."

"Then why wasn't she liked?" Fay asked.

Trixie thought of her sensible banker father. If Peter Belden had been living in that long-ago time, she was sure that somehow he would have found a way to put a stop to the rumors and gossip that had ended in tragedy at Lisgard House.

"One year," Trixie said slowly, "everything was going wrong for the townspeople of Sleepyside. Crops that had been planted wouldn't grow. Cattle got sick and died. And then some children in town started getting sick, too—and several of them died, as well."

Fay drew in her breath sharply. "What sickness was it?"

"Nobody knows for sure," Trixie replied. "Dad thinks it could have been an outbreak of scarlet fever. Or maybe it was diphtheria or whooping cough. Brian told me that diseases like those were very serious in those days. People didn't have the drugs we have today, of course."

"And so, when the children died, they blamed Sarah Sligo?" Fay asked.

Trixie nodded. "Yes, they blamed Sarah. You know, she must have been an obstinate sort of person. She wouldn't listen to the more level-headed townspeople, who tried to warn her that feelings were running high against her."

"She kept on wearing her funny-looking clothes," Honey said. "And she kept on wandering around the marsh, collecting whatever it was she collected."

"So on Thanksgiving night," Trixie continued,

her voice low, "a group of angry people got together and made their way here, to her house."

Trixie stopped, listening. In her imagination, she could almost see the long, flickering torches illuminating the hands and angry faces of the people who carried them. She could almost hear the roar of the mob as they reached the front door of the Lisgard mansion.

"They broke through the entrance," Trixie said, "and they found Sarah waiting for them in one of the rooms—the room you showed us, I guess, Fay—" She hesitated.

"Go on, Trix," Honey whispered, "though I don't like this next bit."

"Sarah Sligo tried to reason with them," Trixie said, trying to make her voice sound matter-of-fact, "but the people were past reason. They accused her of everything they could think of, and when they had finished, they locked her up in that little room. They boarded up the window so she couldn't get out. And then they set fire to the house."

There was silence.

"And so Sarah Sligo died," Fay said at last.

"Yes."

"And the ghost?" Fay's voice was low. "What about the ghost?"

Trixie moved restlessly. "I wouldn't worry

57

about it, Fay," she said hurriedly. "I expect it's just one of those silly stories that get passed around when people have nothing better to do."

Honey clasped her hands around her bent knees and glanced across at their new friend. "You've never seen a ghost here, have you, Fay?" she asked.

Fay didn't seem to be listening. It was as if she were following some thought of her own. All at once, she lifted her head and gazed steadily at Trixie. "And now tell me about the curse," she said softly.

Trixie had been half prepared for this particular question and had already decided not to answer it. "I don't know anything about a curse, Fay," she lied blandly.

Honey's eyes opened wide. "Why, Trix! You do, too! You told me that before she died, Sarah Sligo swore she would get her revenge. She placed a curse on this house and on everyone who would ever live in it—" She stopped in horror, clapping a hand to her mouth.

"It's all right, Honey," Fay said quietly. "I only needed someone to confirm what I already knew."

"What do you know, Fay?" Trixie asked.

Fay bit her lip. "I know that it's bad luck to live in this house," she replied. "I know that the first Lisgard who ever lived here went walking in the marsh one day and was never seen again. I know there was something funny about the death of the last owner, old Caleb Lisgard—"

Honey frowned. "I hadn't heard that. What sort of something funny?"

"I'm not sure," Fay answered, "but everyone in town has been talking about it for weeks."

Trixie made a mental note to ask Brian later. Perhaps he'd heard something about it.

"And what's more," Fay continued, "we—my mother and I—haven't had much luck lately, either. Last week I almost fell as I was coming downstairs. And now tonight"—her eyes filled with tears—"Mother's in the hospital with a broken hip."

Both Trixie and Honey scrambled out of bed and hurried to Fay's side.

"You mustn't listen to stupid stories about this house anymore," Trixie said firmly.

"And I shouldn't have told you about the curse," Honey added, looking as if she was close to tears herself. She put her arm around her new friend. "I'm sure that your mother merely had a nasty accident. It didn't have anything to do with this house, or any stupid old curse, or any silly old witch."

"Honey's right," Trixie said. "There're lots and lots of stories about spooky happenings in this part of the world. We've even had some spooky adventures, ourselves. For instance, did we ever tell you about the night we met a headless horseman in the woods?" She wiggled her eyebrows at Honey.

"Oh, sure," Honey said, realizing that Trixie wanted to distract Fay from her fears. "Then there was the time when we saw a ghostly galleon near an old pirate's hideaway."

Fay looked from one to the other. "A headless horseman?" she echoed. "A ghostly galleon?"

Honey nodded. "Would you like us to tell you about them?"

Fay moved her legs to make room for the two friends on her bed. "I know what you're doing," she said, smiling through her tears, "and you're very kind. So, yes, I'd like to hear about them."

"And when we've finished those," Honey said with satisfaction, "remind me to tell you of the times we discovered an abandoned baby and searched for a phantom grasshopper!"

It was very late when Honey finished the last exciting story. Fay was already yawning, and politely trying to hide the fact, while Trixie's legs had long since gone to sleep. The rest of her was ready to join them.

"Would you like me to tell you now about the time Trixie saw a shark in the Hudson River?" Honey asked, still anxious to make amends for upsetting Fay in the first place.

She seemed greatly relieved when their new friend assured her that any more stories could wait until the following morning.

Almost before Trixie and Fay had had time to blink, Honey had hurried to her own bed, had pulled the covers up to her chin, and was snuggling deep into her pillow.

"I am a little tired," she said apologetically and closed her eyes. Soon she was breathing deeply.

"Is she asleep?" Fay asked softly.

Trixie chuckled. "I'd say she's good for at least eight hours." She smoothed the blankets on the old armchair, then climbed between them once more.

"Good night, Trixie, and thank you," Fay called quietly as she reached for the light switch beside her bed. "Are you sure you're comfortable? Would you like to change places with me?"

"Don't worry," Trixie said, yawning. "It doesn't matter to me where I sleep, and tonight I won't need any rocking. I'm much too tired."

Fay sighed. "I wish I were. As it is, I'm sure I'm going to do nothing but wonder how Mother is doing at the hospital, and, what's more. . . ."

Fay stopped talking.

Trixie frowned and raised herself up onto one elbow. "And? Fay? And what?"

There was no answer. All Trixie could hear was the rhythmic sound of deep, heavy breathing. And now it came not only from Honey's bed, but from Fay's as well.

Trixie chuckled, tucked her legs under her, shifted her pillow, and settled herself down to sleep.

Ten minutes later, she realized that the armchair was just as uncomfortable as Fay had guessed it would be. No matter which way she turned, a part of Trixie stuck over or under a part of the chair.

Too, she had to admit to herself that she was worried. There was something about their new friend that made Trixie feel uneasy. It was as if Fay were hiding something—some knowledge that she didn't yet want to share.

It was certainly unfortunate that Fay had already learned of the curse of Lisgard House. It had seemed to upset her, Trixie thought.

She sighed, turned over, and for the tenth time, rearranged the blankets that kept slipping to the floor.

Again and again, Trixie's thoughts returned to the strange figure she'd seen outside the house. She remembered the mysterious voice she'd heard when she stood alone in the kitchen. *Who or what was it?*

All at once, Trixie remembered something else and sat bolt upright. She had meant to see if the back door was locked and bolted.

In another instant, she had slipped from between the blankets and was feeling her way along the dark passage toward the back door.

She thought at first that her eyes had become adjusted extra quickly to the gloom around her. Then she realized that there was a dim, shimmering light coming from the open kitchen door off the passage.

When she poked her head around it to see, she noticed that Fay had failed to turn off a small light over the stove.

Trixie meant to go and turn it off, but at that moment, there was a small movement in the hallway behind her.

She gasped and, whirling toward it, saw a sight that took her breath away.

A strange figure stood by the back door. The outlines of it were fuzzy, almost as if Trixie were seeing it through some sort of distorted lens.

It wore a tall, pointed hat. It wore a black cloak that reached almost to the floor.

As Trixie watched, frozen to the spot, it raised an arm. Trixie saw one long, bony finger pointing straight at her.

Then the terrible figure spoke.

"Beware!" it whispered. *"Beware!"*

And then it vanished.

Trixie took a faltering step forward—and screamed at the top of her lungs.

Night of Terror! • 5

BACK IN FAY'S ROOM only minutes later, Trixie was still struggling to recover her composure as her two worried friends watched her anxiously.

"I still don't understand what happened, Trix," Honey declared, looking down at her friend as she sat on the edge of Fay's bed. "One minute I was sound asleep, and the next minute, I thought the roof was falling in."

"You still haven't told us why you screamed like that," said Fay, who was seated beside Trixie. "What happened? What frightened you? Was it—" she hesitated—"something you heard?"

Trixie wished that she could stop trembling and

made another valiant effort to do so. "N-No," she said uncertainly. "It—it wasn't what I heard—or, at least, not *just* what I heard. It was something I thought I saw." She frowned and pressed her hands together to try to prevent them from shaking. They felt as though they'd turned into two lumps of ice. She moistened her dry lips with the tip of her tongue. "Of course, I couldn't have seen what I thought I saw. What I thought I saw was something that nobody in their right mind could see. So I couldn't have seen it, do you see?"

"No," Honey said flatly. "I haven't got the faintest idea what you're talking about." She moved to Trixie's armchair-bed, sat down, and tucked her legs under her. "Begin with why you were out of bed in the first place."

Trixie shot an apologetic look at Fay, who was, she thought, looking as upset and as apprehensive as Trixie felt.

"I went to see if the back door was locked," Trixie said in a rush.

Fay looked surprised. "Why, thank you, Trixie," she said. "That was thoughtful of you. But you didn't need to worry, you know. That door works on a spring lock. Mother and I don't bother about bolting that one because we know it can only be opened with a key. If only I'd known you were worried about it, I could have told you.

Naturally, we always make sure the other outside windows and doors are safe from intruders. We don't want anyone bursting in on us unannounced, either."

Trixie sighed. Why didn't she ever give anyone else credit for a little common sense? Why did she always assume that she was the only one who had the bright ideas?

One of these days, Trixie Belden, she thought gloomily, *you're going to realize that you're not nearly as smart as you think you are. Next time Mart calls you a pea-brain, don't be so quick to disagree with him. He might be right!*

She jumped to her feet and began pacing up and down in the small space between the two beds. "I should have known there was nothing to worry about," she said at last. "Anyway, I'd got as far as the kitchen when I noticed we'd left a light burning there. It must have happened when we were making that hot chocolate, I think. So I was about to go in and turn off the light, when—"

She stopped suddenly as she caught sight of her new friend. Fay's face was white as she looked up at Trixie. Her dark brown eyes looked anxious and fearful.

Trixie was about to rush on impulsively with her story, when she noticed that, unconsciously, Fay was wringing her hands. She couldn't help herself. She was actually wringing her hands!

Trixie had often read about fictional characters who did that, but she didn't remember ever seeing a real, live person do it.

Fay's hands clutched each other nervously. Their fingers intertwined, then released their grip. Each hand "washed" the other, then clutched at the other once more. Fay did it over and over.

Trixie thought back over the events of the evening. She recalled how hard Fay had tried to conceal her worry about her mother's accident. She remembered Fay's reaction to that small room off the living room that had been the scene of the long-ago tragedy. She remembered Fay's intense, almost unnatural, interest in Sarah Sligo's story.

"Yes?" Fay prompted her. "You were about to go into the kitchen and turn off the light when you saw—what?"

"A mouse," Trixie said, crossing her fingers behind her back. Surely it wouldn't matter if she told another small lie if, by doing so, she would protect a friend in trouble.

Honey stared. "You—you saw a *mouse?* Do you mean to tell me that was what all this—" she waved a hand in the direction of her warm and comfortable bed—"is about?"

Trixie swung around to face her. "It—uh—startled me," she finished lamely.

Fay sighed and seemed to relax at once. "Is that all it was? I thought—that is— Maybe it was just a little field mouse from the marsh you saw, Trixie," she said. "We do get them sometimes. When we can catch them, Mother and I always put them back outside where they came from."

Trixie nodded her curly head vigorously. "Yes, that's what it must have been—a field mouse from the marsh. It was white and brown and had a little pink, twitchy nose."

Honey was far from satisfied. "I still don't understand it," she declared. "You've never been scared of a mouse in your life, Trixie Belden. In fact, one time you told me you thought they were cute."

"They are cute," Trixie replied firmly, "but not at this time of the night—morning, I mean. Gleeps! Look at the time. We'll never get any sleep at this rate."

Still talking, she shooed Honey back to her own bed and stood over Fay as she swung her slim legs back under the covers. In another few moments, Trixie had arranged herself, if not comfortably, then at least in a position in which she thought she could sleep.

When Fay turned out the light once more, however, Trixie found that her brain was just as active as it had been earlier.

She tried to remember every single detail of the apparition she had seen in the hallway—if, indeed, it had been an apparition at all. Had she seen the witch's ghost? Had Sarah Sligo appeared in order to warn her of another impending tragedy? If so, what tragedy? And when was it supposed to happen?

On the other hand, it could have been someone playing a trick on her. But how had it been accomplished? The more Trixie thought about it, the more she was certain that the figure in the hallway had not been anything like the one she'd seen outside the house. The one outside had been real and solid, while the figure in the hallway—

Trixie gasped and sat bolt upright in bed. What she had been about to say to herself was that the figure in the passage had been transparent.

Trixie had been able to see right through it!

Later, Trixie could have sworn that she hadn't closed her eyes even for a second. It had seemed to her that after her last startling thought, she was so wide-awake that she never expected to close her eyes again.

Whatever the truth of the matter, the next thing she knew was that someone was shaking her. Trixie tried to bury her nose deeper in her pillow.

"Go 'way!" she mumbled. "I'm only waiting till

Fay's asleep. Then I'm going to wake Honey up, and we're both going hunting for that ghost."

"What ghost?" Honey's voice said in her ear. "Oh, please, wake up, Trix! Listen, can't you hear it?"

At first, Trixie could hear nothing but the beating of her own heart. Then, as if from a great distance, she could hear the sound of marching feet, and the sound of angry voices. They grew louder.

Every nerve in Trixie's body seemed to snap to attention. Her eyes, which, until this moment, she hadn't known were closed, popped open. She turned her head and gazed up at the white blob that was Honey's face bending over her in the dark.

Trixie gasped and sat up. As she did so, Fay snapped on the light and stared, white-faced, across the room at them.

"What was that?" she asked in terror.

As if in answer, fists pounded at the front door. "Open up!" a man's rough voice roared. "We know you're in there! Open up!"

Trixie leaped from her nest of blankets and stood quivering, every muscle alert. She stared toward Fay's bedroom door as if, by her will alone, she could see through it.

Fists continued to pound on that distant front entrance. Now the first voice was joined by others.

They were angry voices—hateful and hate-filled.

Soon Trixie fancied she could hear other feet tramping across gravel and onto the porch. As she strained her ears, she could detect a low persistent muttering. It sounded just like the noise of an unruly mob.

"I don't believe it," she said, staring at her friends with wide eyes, "but it's almost as if we're reliving the death of Sarah Sligo!"

Fay and Honey were beyond speech. They stared back at her in horror.

In the next instant, it seemed that strong axes were biting into wood. Somewhere a door had burst open, as if made of cardboard. The sound of angry voices grew louder—and closer.

"Come out, you witch!"

"Find her!"

"Kill her! Kill her! Kill her!"

Then there was silence.

The three girls stared toward the bedroom door.

A long moment passed. Finally, her voice trembling, Honey asked, "Is—is it over?"

"Oh, please, please let it be over." Fay's eyes were closed. She was kneeling in bed, hugging her arms across her chest and rocking herself back and forth.

"Stop it, Fay!" Trixie's voice was sharp. "Come on! We've got to get out of here, now! I have a feeling that this—this—whatever it is—isn't over at all. If we're fast, we can run before it starts again."

She ran to the door and reached for the knob. But it was too late.

Someone in the passage outside was shuffling slowly toward their room—and the someone was moaning!

"Come on!" Trixie yelled and yanked at the door.

"We're ready, Trix!" Honey gasped from behind her.

Fay was sobbing, her hands clutching Trixie's outstretched arm. "Open it!" she screamed. "What are you waiting for? Let's get out of this dreadful place."

Trixie turned to face them, her face white. "We can't get out of here," she answered deliberately. "We seem to be locked in!"

The next few minutes were a haze of terror for the three friends. The footsteps shuffled closer and closer toward them. The moans grew louder, as if the person making them were in agony.

Then they heard the voice, begging, pleading with them to open the door.

"Let me in!" the voice screamed. "For pity's sake, do something. Help me! Oh, help me!"

Next, Trixie heard the terrible sound of frantic

fingernails scrabbling over woodwork. Then some-one's fists pounded against their door—and pounded—and pounded—

Trixie backed away in horror. "We—we can't let you in!" she shouted at last. "We're locked in ourselves!"

"Go away!" Fay screamed.

"Leave us alone!" Honey yelled.

For a moment, all noises stopped. Then some-one laughed softly.

"Then open thy ears and listen well," a voice whispered. "Thou thought to burn me—and may-hap thou hast! But curses be upon thy heads—yea, even unto thy children and thy children's children. Thou wilt be sorry for thy actions this night. Burn me, would ye? Then watch!"

The voice stopped, but the three girls couldn't move. It was as if they were frozen with terror.

"Oh, Trix," Honey cried, clutching her friend with both hands, "what does it all mean? What is it we have to watch for?"

Trixie's face was grim as she stared at the floor. She pointed. "There!" she said, her voice shaking. "That's what we have to watch for!"

Unbelievably, a curl of black smoke was billow-ing toward them from beneath the door.

"The house is on fire!" Fay screamed.

Helpless, she and Honey watched as Trixie

twisted and tugged and yanked desperately at the knob once more.

"It won't budge!" Trixie shouted.

The smoke, thicker now, stung her eyes and choked her lungs. She gazed frantically about her.

But no window had appeared magically since the last time she'd looked. The walls, with their brave display of bright mementos, offered no other exit. The room had become a prison from which there was no escape.

Trixie turned to her friends. "It's no use," she said hopelessly, her voice catching on a sob. "We're trapped! And, like Sarah Sligo, we're going to be burned alive!"

The Odd Odd-Job Man · 6

GASPING FOR AIR, Trixie and her friends huddled together in horror on Fay's bed. They clutched each other for comfort as the choking smoke billowed toward them.

Suddenly, outside the door, someone screamed. Then there was silence.

It seemed that that terrible scream still hung in the air as Trixie strained her ears to listen. She expected still to hear the muffled roar of an angry mob. She wouldn't have been surprised to hear muffled footsteps moving haltingly back along that dark passage.

But she heard nothing.

Puzzled, Trixie turned her head toward the room's only exit. She expected to see long orange tongues of flame reaching under it to consume her, the way they had reached out to consume the witch, Sarah Sligo.

But again, she saw nothing.

Even the smoke had stopped belching. As she watched, the choking fog seemed to lift, slowly at first, and then faster. It was as if someone had opened an outside door to let in the blessed fresh air.

Trixie reached out and shook Honey and Fay, who were still clutching each other convulsively. "It's the weirdest thing," she said slowly, "but I think we're saved."

Honey moaned. "You're just saying that to make us feel better, Trix."

Fay's eyes were closed and she was gasping for air. "You're wrong, Trixie," she whispered. "You must be. How can we be saved when we're about to be burned to death?"

"See for yourself," Trixie told them as she moved stiffly away. She clambered off the bed and stood still, looking about her.

There was no question about it now. The haze of smoke still hung in the air, but it was less— much less. Around her, the house was quiet, as if it were exhausted.

Trixie moved to the door and stretched out a trembling hand toward it. The knob twisted easily under her grasp.

She hesitated, afraid to look into the passage outside. What terrible sight would meet her eyes? Would she see the still body of a figure dressed in a black hat and a flowing cloak? Would the dreadful specter be burned beyond all recognition?

Trixie gasped at the very thought and snatched her hand away from the door.

Honey had been watching. "What is it, Trix?" she asked, her voice shaking. "Is—is the door still locked? Will we have to stay here forever?"

Trixie's mouth felt dry. Her throat burned painfully. "I was thinking—that is—what do you think we're going to find once we open that door? Oh, and by the way, it isn't locked now."

"Then open it," Fay whispered.

Slowly, cautiously, Trixie's hand moved toward the knob once more. At that moment, she thought she heard the faint click of a spring lock moving quietly into place.

Trixie flung open the bedroom door and stared straight ahead of her. She saw only the dim outlines of the passage outside. Gathering all her courage, she stepped across the threshold and glanced quickly at the back door. She had the feeling that it was this lock she'd heard closing.

She was afraid to turn her head and look the other way, toward the front of the house. How far had the fire reached? Was it even now creeping toward her defenseless back? If so, why didn't she feel the fire's heat? Why hadn't the doorknob felt hot under her fingers? Why was it so icy-cold here in the passage?

Above all, where would she find the body?

At last, she turned and looked. She rubbed her eyes and looked again.

There was nothing.

No fire licked its way along the passage toward her. No inert body lay like a bag of old laundry on the floor.

A haze of lingering smoke hovered outside Fay's bedroom door. But it was the only sign that anything at all had happened that night.

"Come quickly!" Trixie told her two friends and beckoned to them to follow her.

Moments later, they stood in the entrance hall and stared about them in disbelief. The front doors, still locked and bolted, stood unmarked. No axes had marred their surface. No hinges hung drunkenly to testify to a shouting mob's rage.

Over her friends' strong objections, Trixie insisted on searching, first the downstairs, then the upstairs, for any sign of the source of the fire. She didn't find any.

"I simply don't understand it!" she exclaimed to Honey some ten minutes later. "It's just as if nothing happened—nothing at all. Pinch me and tell me if I've been dreaming all this time."

"I don't have to pinch you," Honey said slowly. "I'm telling you. It all happened."

"Then where's the evidence?" Trixie asked, trying to sound reasonable.

"The evidence is here," Fay's voice said from behind them.

They turned to see her standing, white-faced, in front of the big entrance doors. Her fists were clenched tightly at her sides.

Trixie frowned. "Well? I don't see anything—only you."

Fay swallowed hard. "I know," she answered slowly. "That's just it. *I'm* the evidence. You—you can blame me for everything. You see, it's all my fault. I—I wasn't sure before, but now I am."

Trixie stared. "I don't understand. What is it you're sure of?"

"I'm possessed," Fay said simply.

"Possessed by what?" Honey asked, sounding as bewildered as Trixie felt.

"It's been going on for some time," Fay said, as if she hadn't heard Honey's question. "I haven't told anybody—not anybody. At first I thought it was all my imagination. I kept on hearing things,

things that no one else seemed to notice."

By now she was crying, and her whole body shook with sobs.

"It's all right, Fay," Trixie said, hurrying to her side. "It's all right. We'll look after you, won't we, Honey?"

"Of course we will." Honey stopped, thinking. "Listen, Trix, one thing's for sure. I've had enough of this house to last me a lifetime. I know it's late, but let's call Brian. He'll come and get us and take us to your house—"

Trixie frowned. "That's no good. The phone's out of order here. Don't you remember? Now I'm wondering what happened to it."

Fay tried to choke back her sobs. "It's nothing spooky, if that's what you mean," she said at last. "The storm last night knocked down a line, that's all. But—but the phone won't be fixed till tomorrow. Oh, Trixie, Honey, what are we going to do?"

Trixie didn't hesitate. "We'll walk home," she stated, "and from here on out, Fay, antiques or no antiques, you're staying at Crabapple Farm until your mother's out of the hospital." Her face was grim. "As for that other thing you just told us— about being possessed, I mean—"

"You can tell us about it later," Honey finished.

"But we *will* help you, Fay," Trixie said, not

really knowing whether she and Honey would be able to. Fay's problem seemed to be getting far beyond their experience.

At first she thought that Fay was going to refuse to move from her position by the front door. It was as if, having begun to tell them her terrible secret, she couldn't rest until she'd told them all of it.

But with Honey helping her, Trixie urged Fay back to that small bedroom where they had spent so many horrifying minutes. This time they made sure that the door was wide open as they dressed.

Then Trixie and Fay, almost without thinking, grabbed a handful of Fay's clothes and flung them into a suitcase. Then, thankfully, they made their way out of the house.

Trixie didn't even begin to breathe easier until they were standing at the mansion's rear gates.

"What are you girls doing out here at this time of night?" a man's rough voice asked suddenly from behind them.

Startled, Fay smothered a scream, Honey jumped nervously, and Trixie swung around and gazed up at a tall figure that had appeared noiselessly out of the shadows.

Shaggy black eyebrows hung over a pair of cold gray eyes. The figure's face, long creased with small wrinkles, was topped by an untidy mane of white hair that fell in ringlets over his ears.

Trixie swallowed hard as she noticed what he was wearing. His painter's overalls, which once could have been white, seemed to be stained with dark splotches of—could it be blood?

Without thinking, Trixie stepped away from him, even though she knew who he was. Zeke Collins, the odd-job man at Lisgard House, had been a resident of Sleepyside for as long as she could remember.

She stared now at those dark stains and wondered if, perhaps, he had managed to trap some small, defenseless creature from the swamp and had been busy butchering it.

She shuddered. "We—my friends and I—are on our way to my house," she stammered at last. "We—we were going to spend the night here—"

"But something happened," Fay added.

"It was the witch, wasn't it?" Zeke Collins said.

Honey gasped. "How did you know?"

Zeke Collins rasped a thumb across a stubble of beard on his chin. "Aye, there ain't much that goes on around here I don't know about," he said, almost to himself. "What was it this time? Did Sarah make an appearance?" He stared from one to the other of them. "I'll tell you straight, some-one's doin' something to upset Sarah. Someone's calling her back from her grave. I don't like it,

I tell you. I don't like it at all. . . ."

Fay looked as if she was about to faint.

"We're going home," Trixie said firmly. "Come on, Fay, Honey. Good night, Mr. Collins."

Zeke Collins didn't move. "It's almost like it was in the old days," he muttered. "There's black magic around, and that's bad news."

Trixie swung open the gate and pulled her friends after her. "Good night," she called again over her shoulder. She could sense that the old man was still staring after them.

"You mark my words," he shouted suddenly. "Whoever it is who's disturbing the haunt—aye, and there is a haunt to disturb—is going to be sorry. There's an evil spirit in that house, and her name is Sarah Sligo. You hear me?"

By the time Trixie and her friends had reached Glen Road and were hurrying along it, some of the night's terrors seemed to be nothing but a bad dream—a nightmare from which they had at last awakened.

The streetlights threw the girls' shadows ahead of them, making them appear as if they were giants out for a stroll. The shadows shortened, vanished under their feet as each lamp was reached, then lengthened again behind them.

Trixie could hear the small sounds of the night life around them as tiny creatures scurried through wild underbrush searching for food. In the distance, getting fainter with each step, the marsh frogs kept up their plaintive croaking.

Trixie could hear Honey and Fay talking in low tones beside her. But she wasn't listening. Her mind was busy, trying to recall every detail of the horrifying night's events. She remembered, too, the confession Fay had been about to make when it was all over.

What had she meant when she'd said she was possessed? Was it possible that Sarah Sligo had somehow taken over Fay's body and was now trying to work her evil once more?

Trixie had no answers to any of these questions. "But just wait till morning," she muttered to herself, "and then I'm going to try to find out everything there is to know."

All the same, she couldn't help wondering where the knowledge would lead her.

Dark Suspicions · 7

IF YOU REALLY WANT to know what I think about your mind-boggling and mystifying adventures last night," Mart said for the third time, "I think that with a small amount of cogitation—if you are still capable of it, Trix—you'll come to the same sane and sensible conclusion that I have reached myself." He took a deep breath. "In other words, sister mine, you were dreaming."

Trixie glared at him across the breakfast table. "We *weren't dreaming*, my dear little *twin* brother. You can ask Honey."

Mart reddened and looked annoyed, as he always did when Trixie reminded him that he was only eleven months older than she was.

He forked up the last bite of blueberry waffle from his plate and popped it into his mouth. "Me mmf mewy wiff monk merfy," he said.

"If you wouldn't talk with your mouth full," Trixie told him, "maybe I could understand what you're saying."

Mart chewed, swallowed, took a long sip from his milk glass, and leaned back in his chair. "Ah, that's better," he announced, patting his stomach. He cocked an eyebrow at Trixie. "What I said was that I can't very well ask Honey. She took Fay over to Manor House to show her around there. So until I receive definite confirmation of your hair-raising tale, my considered opinion, previously stated, remains unchanged." He looked across the table at Brian. "What do you think?"

Brian had been listening quietly to their conversation. "You have to admit, Trix," he said at last, "that the whole thing sounds crazy. You woke Mart and me up in the middle of the night to let you in. You promised to tell us all about it this morning—"

"Which I've done," Trixie put in.

"—but it still doesn't make sense," Brian continued. "Mart and I were talking about it after you three had gone upstairs to bed." He stared at her curiously. "How did three of you ever manage to fit into two beds, by the way?"

"Very carefully," Trixie answered absently.

Although the Beldens had a guest room downstairs, Trixie hadn't even thought of asking either Fay or Honey to sleep in it when they all reached Crabapple Farm the previous night. After their terrible experiences at Lisgard House, it was as if the three of them had an unspoken agreement to stay together and offer comfort to each other.

Trixie had wondered if Fay would want to stay up and talk for a while. But she hadn't. Her face, still white and drawn, had a strange, stricken look to it, almost as if she'd had more than she could bear for one day.

And so, carefully avoiding the subject that was foremost in their minds, Trixie and Honey had insisted that she should rest. Although Fay had told them that she knew she would not be able to close her eyes for the rest of the night, it hadn't been five minutes before she was fast asleep. Soon Trixie and Honey were, too.

In the cold light of that Saturday morning, however, the events of the previous night seemed somehow less terrifying. Now that Trixie had had a chance to think about them, she was sure there was some sensible, believable explanation for what had happened.

"You know what I think?" she said suddenly. "I

think someone's trying to scare Fay into having a nervous breakdown."

Brian shifted uneasily in his chair. "Now, come on," he said. "You've got no reason to believe anything like that. What on earth gave you such an idea?"

"Figure it out for yourselves," Trixie told her brothers. "When I got to the house last night, I thought I saw someone outside. That was the first thing."

Brian nodded. "That was Zeke Collins."

"Maybe it was, and maybe it wasn't," Trixie replied. "But then there was the other stuff. I heard someone telling me to beware. And then— and then—"

"You thought you saw a ghost," Mart said.

Trixie nodded. "I thought I did, really. I—I know it sounds silly."

"Wow! What an understatement!" Mart leaned across the table toward her. "Did it occur to you that it could have been either Fay or Honey perpetrating a peculiar practical joke?"

Trixie flushed. "That's *really* silly," she said with conviction. "They were asleep. Anyway, neither of them would do such a thing."

Brian frowned. "I think you're right, Trix," he said, "at least as far as Honey is concerned. But what about Fay?"

"What about her?" Trixie demanded. She stared at him, puzzled.

Her eldest brother played idly with his fork and, with the handle of it, drew lines on the tablecloth. "None of us know Fay that well," he said slowly. "I was wondering whether she might have been behind all the strange things you say you saw and heard last night."

Trixie felt bewildered. "But why?"

Brian shrugged. "Beats me. The whole thing sounds funny, that's all. You heard people arriving at the house, you said. They were angry and shouting. Then you say they broke down the front door with axes. After that there was the business with the smoke. But when you came to look afterward, everything was normal. The door *hadn't* been broken into, there *wasn't* a fire—"

"Fay could have cooked up the whole thing," Mart said. "Maybe she needed you there as witnesses. Maybe she was trying to turn your tumultuous tresses to silver."

Before Trixie could come up with a retort, Brian put in, "He means she was trying to turn your hair gray."

"Or maybe," Mart said thoughtfully, "she knew that you are constantly panting after problematical predicaments—mysteries to you, Trix—and she decided to provide you with one."

Trixie pushed back her chair and stood up. "That's stupid," she snapped, her blue eyes blazing. "I thought you two would be able to help. I should have known better. Fay's in trouble, real trouble."

Brian looked up at her and asked, "What did Dad say about all this?"

Trixie had the grace to blush. "I—uh—didn't tell him—that is, not everything."

"Why not?" Mart demanded.

Trixie looked down at her feet. "I didn't want to worry him and Moms," she said, "so I just told both of them that Fay's mother had an accident, and that we'd been planning to spend the night at Lisgard House, but then we'd decided to come back here, instead."

"Did you tell them what time you arrived home?" Brian asked. He frowned up at her. "It wasn't the smartest idea in the world to walk home alone at two o'clock in the morning, you know."

"To say nothing about throwing pebbles up at our window," Mart added. "You nearly scared us out of half a year's growth."

Trixie glared at him. "It would take a lot to scare you out of any growth, Mart Belden," she retorted, "especially out this way." She made a large circle of her arms and then extended them

91

outward beyond the region of her stomach.

Brian chuckled. "She's got you there, Mart. If you don't stop eating, one of these days we'll be calling you Mr. Five-by-Five."

"I'd rather be called Five-by-Five than Two-by-Four," Mart answered blandly. As his brother and sister raised their eyebrows, puzzled, he added, "That's the size of Trixie's brain—in centimeters, that is."

Furious, Trixie was about to snap back at him, when she remembered her resolution of the night before. Instead, she contented herself with giving him a superior, tolerant look. "At the height of last night's—uh—confusion," she said at last, "I made up my mind that the next time you called me a pea-brain, Mart, I would agree with you."

"Such humility is astonishing!" Mart declared at once. "And to what circumstance do we owe such an astounding reversal of your self-esteem?"

Trixie looked down at her hands. "I was wondering if Fay had locked up the house," she said, her voice low. "She had."

Mart pushed back his chair and stood up. "That seems to settle that, then," he said, the teasing note gone from his voice. "If no one could get into the house, Trix, then it *had* to be either Fay or Honey perpetrating a particularly putrid practical joke. We've already agreed that Honey wouldn't do such a thing. So guess which one that leaves."

"Oh, Mart, I'm sure Fay wouldn't do such a thing," Trixie said slowly, but she didn't sound as certain as she had before.

Mart pushed back his chair and strolled to the refrigerator. He paused with his hand on the door. "Mind you, I'm not saying Fay *did* do the dirty deed. Never let it be said that I'd think evil of an honored houseguest, but—" he paused—"we don't know that much about her, you know. She might be playing some game we know nothing about. I'd be careful if I were you. And I certainly wouldn't go anywhere near that spooky old house again, if I could help it."

Trixie didn't look at him. "Umm—that's the next thing I was going to tell you. We—that is, Fay and I—have to go back there sometime today."

Brian stared at her. "Trixie! What on earth for?"

"We—umm—that is, we left in such a hurry last night," Trixie said quickly, "that we weren't looking when we grabbed some clothes and flung them into a suitcase. We thought we'd packed what Fay would need for her stay here, but when we put everything away this morning, we—we discovered that we had grabbed all the wrong

93

things for Fay to wear."

Trixie could tell that her brothers had already guessed what she was about to ask next. Brian's next words proved it.

"And so you want us to come with you to pack the right things?" he asked, sounding annoyed.

"Can't you make do with what you've got?" Mart asked. "For crying out loud, what does she need? A couple pairs of jeans, a shirt or two? What did you pack?"

"Bathing suits," Trixie said and looked up at last at her almost-twin. "Why, Mart, what's the matter? Don't you want to visit the haunted house? Are you afraid that Sarah Sligo will turn you into a little green frog and that you will go *ribbit, ribbit, ribbit* forevermore?"

Brian sighed. "Okay, Trix. We'll come with you after I've taken Fay to visit her mother in the hospital. We've called Dr. Ferris, and he said Mrs. Franklin was doing fine, by the way. I told Fay we'd be ready to leave in an hour."

Trixie felt more relieved than she was ready to admit. Although she had been prepared to go with Fay to collect her clothes, she hadn't been looking forward to it one bit. She knew that Honey felt the same way. Perhaps, too, Fay would feel better about explaining her problem to them once she had seen that her mother was really all right.

Only once that morning had Trixie tried to ask about what Fay had wanted to tell them the previous night. But when Trixie mentioned the subject, Fay hadn't wanted to talk about it.

She had merely squeezed Trixie's hand and said, "I'll tell you later, Trixie, honestly I will. But let's just leave it for a while, okay? I—I'm enjoying myself so much here. You have no idea how nice it is to hear a sound overhead and realize it's only Bobby or Reddy or Brian or Mart. I don't have to wonder if it's someone—or something—else." She had paused. "Besides, I'm sure I can trust both you and Honey, but—"

It was then that kindhearted Honey, seeing Fay's discomfort, had offered to show her Manor House and its grounds.

"I should have let her tell me all about it last night," Trixie muttered to herself. "As it is, I'm simply dying of curiosity."

"You usually are," Mart remarked, taking a bowl of apples from the refrigerator and setting it carefully in the center of the table. "And speaking of curiosity, perhaps you, Trixie, can provide your elders and betters with some relief from one minor, but persistent, twinge of guilt experienced by two male members of your clan."

"Oh, Mart!" Trixie exclaimed. "Why can't you ever speak plain English?" She watched him as he

95

reached toward the apple bowl. His hand hovered over it.

She knew him only too well. He had finished his breakfast; now he was ready for a snack!

Brian chuckled and laid down his fork. "Mart means that he and I have been feeling guilty because we walked out on you last night, Trix— before all the excitement began, that is. We were just wondering if you'd finished your homework."

Trixie had a sudden sneaky thought. "Take two apples from three apples, and what do you have?" she asked innocently.

Mart looked puzzled. Then he reached for three apples and lined them up on the table in front of him. "That's easy," he said. He put two apples into Trixie's hands. "Take two apples from three apples, and what do you have?"

Trixie looked at the apple on the table. She sighed. "One apple."

Brian laughed. "Think again, Trix. How many do *you* have?"

A slow grin spread across Trixie's face. "I have *two* apples. No, *Mart* has two apples. He's earned them." She placed them into her almost-twin's hands.

Mart frowned. "I have no conception of what that was all about. The question remains, bird-brain, did you finish your homework?"

Trixie laughed, her worries about her new friend temporarily forgotten. "I have now," she answered, her blue eyes twinkling.

A few moments later, she was on her way to find her mother, when she overheard Mart say, "*Bathing suits?* Did Trixie say they packed *bathing suits?* In *November?* What on earth could they have been thinking of?"

"Probably witches and curses and ghoulies and ghosties and things that go bump in the night," Brian misquoted softly. "You know, Mart, I don't like the sound of any of this. No, I don't like the sound of it at all."

At once, all of Trixie's fears came rushing back. So sensible Brian, too, was worried about the strange happenings at Lisgard House.

"And I don't like the sound of it, either," Trixie muttered softly to herself, suddenly sure there was worse to come.

Is Fay Possessed? · 8

Trixie felt guilty when at last she found her mother. Helen Belden was in the guest room, making sure that everything would be comfortable for Trixie's new friend.

"I thought she'd be more at ease if I put her in here," Mrs. Belden explained as she caught sight of Trixie in the doorway.

Trixie felt her cheeks grow hot. "I meant to tidy up in here, Moms," she said. "I guess I forgot about it. I can do it now, though, if you'd like."

Mrs. Belden smiled at her daughter. "You're too late, dear. It's just about all done. But really, Trixie, I can't think why you didn't let Fay use this room last night. It must have been very uncomfortable with three of you trying to fit into two beds."

"We managed," Trixie answered, remembering how she and Honey had let Fay have one bed to herself, while they shared the other.

She hesitated. "Moms, what do you know about Mrs. Franklin—Fay's mother?"

Mrs. Belden brushed a strand of fair hair away from her pretty face. "Well, I've met her a couple of times in Lytell's store," she answered. "I thought she was a very pleasant person. I invited her here for coffee on a couple of occasions, but each time, something came up and she couldn't come. I do think she's had a difficult time of it, though. It can't be easy trying to raise a child on one's own these days."

"And Fay?" Trixie asked, thinking of her brothers' suspicions. "What do you know about Fay?"

Mrs. Belden looked startled. "Why, you'd know more about her than I would, Trixie. She seems like a nice youngster—a little too pale, perhaps, and certainly too thin." She glanced at Trixie's sturdy figure with satisfaction. "And, of course, I can tell Fay's worried about something. Is—is it anything I can help with, dear?"

Trixie felt a sudden rush of affection and gave her mother a fervent hug. "Thank you, Moms," she said. "I guess we all know we can count on you for just about everything. But I don't think you can help Fay—not just yet, anyway."

Mrs. Belden turned away and straightened the bright quilt on the neat maple bed. "There," she said. "Now, everything's ready for your guest. And, Trixie, I've told her she can stay for as long as she needs to." She sighed. "I keep on thinking how lucky I am. . . ."

Trixie gave her a final hug and turned toward the door. "We're very lucky, too, Moms," she answered. "Now, about those chores you wanted me to do this morning—"

Mrs. Belden laughed. "It's all right, dear. You can run along. Just don't tell your father that I let you off so easily. As for Bobby, you don't even have to worry about baby-sitting with him today. He's gone over to the Lynches' to play with the twins."

Trixie was still smiling to herself as she hurried away to find Honey and Fay. She looked for them first in the Wheeler stable. They weren't there, but she stopped for a moment to pet the soft nose of Susie, the little black mare.

Trixie remembered how she and Honey had bought Susie for Miss Trask, who, with Regan, helped to manage the Wheeler estate.

"Maybe I'll get to ride you later on today,"

Trixie whispered softly in Susie's ear.

Suddenly there was a clattering of hooves in the stable yard outside. A horse whinnied, and a second later, redheaded Regan strode into the stable, leading Jupiter, the Wheelers' big black gelding.

Jupiter's muscles rippled under his shining coat, and Trixie took care to stand well away from his sharp hooves. Although he was one of the most beautiful of horses, he was usually hard to manage.

Today, though, the big horse was behaving himself for once as he allowed Regan to lead him into his stall and slip the saddle from his back.

Regan glanced at Trixie sharply. "Wonders will never cease," he said. "At last a Bob-White has appeared voluntarily to exercise the horses. I waited for either Jim or Brian to show up, but when they didn't, I took Jupe out myself." He reached for a brush and began grooming the gelding.

Trixie flushed. Regan was always complaining, and rightfully, that she and the other Bob-Whites didn't exercise the horses as often as they should.

She felt guilty as she glanced at the other stalls. Besides Susie, there was Strawberry, a roan who was Mart's favorite mount; Starlight, a chestnut gelding, usually ridden by Brian; and Lady, a fine dapple gray mare. Their luminous eyes seemed to

101

stare back at her reproachfully.

"I'll try to get all the Bob-Whites back here this afternoon, Regan," she said hastily. "Honestly, I will. But for right now, I'm looking for Honey and another—uh—friend of mine."

Regan didn't look up. "If the other friend is young Fay Franklin, you'll find 'em both up at the house. They were headed that way not five minutes ago. I think Honey had been showing the Franklin girl the boathouse." He paused, brush in hand. "What's the matter with her, Trixie?"

Trixie pretended to misunderstand. "You mean Honey?"

"Of course I don't mean Honey," Regan replied. "I mean Fay. She seems a nervous sort of young 'un, if you ask me. When I saw them both, I pulled Jupe to a halt and asked her how she liked living in a genuine haunted house. I was only kidding, but I thought she was going to faint." He glanced up at Trixie. "Fay doesn't believe all that baloney about ghosts and curses, does she?"

"I don't know," Trixie answered slowly. Then she remembered the question she'd meant to ask Brian this morning. "Regan, what do you know about old Caleb Lisgard—I mean, about the way he died?"

Regan grunted and began brushing Jupiter's sleek neck in slow, easy strokes. "There's been plenty of gossip about it lately," he admitted, "and some of it, I think, was started by Zeke Collins. He was there when the old man died—at least, that's what Zeke's been telling everyone." He paused, brush in hand. "But then, you can't always believe Zeke's stories. I've often thought he lets his imagination get away from him."

"But what did he say?" Trixie asked.

Regan turned to face her. "If what Zeke says is true, it's the craziest thing I ever heard in my life. He said old Caleb was sitting in his study, working. He heard a noise, looked up, and what do you think he saw? Zeke says it was the ghost of Sarah Sligo."

"The witch again!" Trixie whispered, almost to herself.

Regan nodded. "Yes, the witch. It gave Caleb such a shock to see her that he had a heart attack and died before Dr. Ferris could get there."

Trixie remembered the strange figure she herself had seen in the passage. She shuddered. "How awful!" she gasped.

"It would be if it were true," Regan said, frowning at her, "but don't forget what I just told you. You can't believe every story you hear. I certainly don't. I'm glad to hear that that young Lewis Gregory doesn't believe it anymore, either."

Trixie was startled. "He doesn't?"

Regan shrugged his broad shoulders. "I'm sure he doesn't. There was a time, after he first moved into that house, when everyone thought he was going to sell the place. He'd been listening to local gossip, you see—and Zeke, I'm sure, was still helping the stories along."

"What happened then?" Trixie asked.

"Lewis Gregory got some sense into his head," Regan answered as he turned back to Jupiter. "He obviously decided to hang on to Lisgard House after all, especially when everyone else told him he should." He glanced at her over his shoulder and grinned. "Besides, no one wanted to buy it. It's not in a very good state of repair, you know."

Trixie was convinced that the true reason was that everyone knew about the ghost. She wondered how many other people, besides herself, had seen the apparition. She almost blurted out her story to Regan, but something warned her to hold her tongue.

She moved uneasily. "Do you believe in ghosts, Regan?" she asked him at last.

"No, I don't," he answered bluntly, "and what's more, neither should you. You hear me?"

Trixie could still feel his worried gaze on her back as he stood at the stable's wide doors and then watched her hurry up the hill toward the beautiful house where Honey lived.

Trixie couldn't help wondering what Regan would have said if she *had* told him about their frightening adventure of the previous night. She had an idea he might have said at once that it was someone playing a practical joke. Brian and Mart thought so. And what if they were right?

"Is Fay really in trouble?" she muttered to herself. "Or is she playing some mysterious game of her own? And I wonder what Honey's thinking about all this."

If was Honey herself who provided the answer to the last question as soon as Trixie hurried into the Wheelers' luxurious living room.

Honey had obviously been holding a low-voiced, worried conversation with Jim Frayne, who stood staring down at her as she sat on the couch.

Jim had a funny look on his face, Trixie thought. It was the same skeptical expression that, earlier, she had seen on the faces of her brothers.

"I was beginning to tell Jim about last night, Trix," Honey said, "and he thinks it was a joke. I don't! I think it's serious—more serious than we ever imagined." She watched as Trixie glanced quickly around the room. "It's okay. Fay's not here. She's gone with Miss Trask to look over the house. But I've heard Fay's story, Trix. She suddenly blurted it all out while I was showing her the lake. And it's so serious that I've sent for the rest of the Bob-Whites. I've told them to meet us in the clubhouse in five minutes."

"If what Honey says is true," Jim said, "the whole thing is simply unbelievable."

Trixie looked from one to the other. "What's unbelievable?"

Honey raised her head and looked steadily at her friend. "Fay thinks the witch's spirit has found a new home," she said, her voice low. "She thinks it's found a new body to live in. You see, Trix, Fay thinks that *she* is becoming Sarah Sligo."

An Astonishing Confession · 9

THIRTY MINUTES LATER, in the clubhouse, Trixie felt even more confused than she had before. She guessed that the other Bob-Whites were feeling the same way.

Trixie almost wished that she could be alone for a while—alone to sort out her thoughts. She glanced around the small cottage that had once been the gatehouse of the huge Wheeler estate.

She remembered how hard the Bob-Whites had worked to turn the cottage into a clubhouse they could all be proud of. Neat curtains hung at the windows. Winter and summer sports equipment was stored on tidy shelves: skis, skates, hockey sticks, sleds, pup tents, tennis rackets, and camping gear.

The Bob-Whites were seated on benches at the big table that Brian and Jim had made. Mart, not as handy with carpentry tools as the other boys, had sanded and stained the furniture.

Trixie knew, as did the others, that there were a lot of memories in their clubhouse—memories of other conferences they'd held, other adventures they'd talked about and puzzled over together.

Trixie glanced at the little cottage's dirt floor and remembered when she'd found a diamond embedded there. She looked up and found that Jim was watching her. She flushed and wondered if he was remembering that adventure, too.

"Well, Trix?" he asked, his face still stiff with shock from the strange story they'd just heard. "What do you think? What can we do to help?"

Trixie leaned toward Fay, who was seated next to dark-haired Dan Mangan on the other side of the table. "I was just thinking, Fay," she said. "This old place has heard a lot of stories in its time—but, jeepers, I don't think it's ever heard anything like this."

"I know," Fay said, her voice trembling, "and I don't blame any of you if you think I'm making the whole thing up."

Pretty Diana Lynch said warmly, "But, of

course, we don't think you're making it up, Fay. At least, *I* don't. I've read a lot about stuff like this—where people get possessed by evil spirits, I mean. Some folks think that there *are* such things as ghosts and that they *do* haunt houses."

"But have you ever heard of anything like this?" Trixie asked.

"N-No, not quite like this," Di answered uncertainly. "Tell us again, Fay. How did you say it all started?"

Now that Fay had told her story once, it seemed as if she found it much easier. "Everything was fine when we first moved into Lisgard House," she told them. "My mother was so pleased and happy that she'd found a good job. Mr. Gregory hired her in New York, you know. Did I tell you that?"

"Yes," Dan said, "I guess you did."

Trixie looked at him sharply. He had a strange note in his voice. It was as though he didn't quite believe the story he'd heard, either. Trixie could tell that both Brian and Mart still had doubts. Neither of them was looking directly at Fay. It was as if they didn't want to meet her eyes.

"We needed money," Fay said, sounding suddenly tired. "My mother is insisting I go on to college later, you see, and you know how expensive that is these days. I did plan on applying for scholarships when the time came, but—"

"We get the picture, Fay," Mart said abruptly, staring down at his hands, which were clasped on the table in front of him. "You and your mother needed the money, so when Mr. Gregory offered a housekeeping position in a haunted house, you both jumped at it."

Fay didn't seem to notice the edge in Mart's voice. She shook her dark head. "No, it wasn't quite like that. We didn't know the history of Lisgard House. In fact, we didn't find out about it until we'd moved in. And he was—that is, Mr. Gregory was paying Mother a very good salary. It was certainly better than anything in salary she'd ever received before."

"Didn't that make you suspicious?" Brian asked.

"No," Fay answered simply. "We just figured our luck had changed for the better at last." She frowned. "I can't really remember when all the strange things began happening. At first it was just little things. It would be stuff like vases moved out of place when I knew I'd put them somewhere else. Once I found all the saucepans and kettles piled in the middle of the kitchen floor."

Honey gasped. "You didn't tell us that before."

Fay moved uneasily in her seat. "There were so many things," she replied. "It's hard to remember all of them. There was that time about a month ago, when we had another storm. Do you

110

remember that? It knocked down a power line that fed electricity to the house. I had to go around lighting candles until the workmen came the next day to fix everything."

Trixie nodded, remembering that October storm. "We lost all our power, too," she said. "We had to use candles, too."

"But mine wouldn't stay lit," Fay said, her voice beginning to shake again. "As fast as I lit them and moved to another room to light others, I'd come back and find that they'd been blown out—or, at least, extinguished."

"Maybe you set them in a draft," Mart suggested, still not looking at her.

"No." Fay sounded certain about it.

"Go on," Trixie prompted her.

"It was soon after this that the strange noises began. I'd hear footsteps upstairs, pacing up and down. And I'd hear doors closing and opening. Once I heard someone laughing, as if there were some sort of joke going on that I knew nothing about. At first I thought it *was* someone playing a joke—"

"A logical and entirely commendable thought," Mart put in.

"I thought it was Zeke Collins," Fay stated flatly. "I thought he might be trying to scare Mother and me away from the house for some reason.

He—he always seems so unfriendly. He's been there for so long, you see. He knows every inch of the grounds. I guess Old Caleb wasn't an easy man to work for. But for some reason, Zeke stayed around, even after the last of the Lisgards died. I think—that is, I thought Zeke wanted the Lisgard place to himself." She tried to laugh. "Mother's convinced that Zeke's got something hidden on the grounds. Buried treasure, maybe. Oh, I know it sounds silly—"

Trixie groaned to herself. It sounded more than silly. It sounded downright unbelievable. She couldn't blame Brian, Mart, and Dan for sounding skeptical. She wasn't surprised when she saw them exchanging doubtful glances.

Fay hurried to finish her story. She told them about all the other strange things that had happened in that old house. She spoke of cold air that seemed to flow through a closed and windowless room. She told of a message written in crayon that she had found scrawled across her dressing table mirror.

"What did it say?" Honey asked, though she'd already heard this part once.

"It said, 'I'm back!' " Fay answered.

"That's all?" Di asked. "Just that? 'I'm back'?"

Brian raised his head at last and looked directly at the Beldens' houseguest. "And what did your mother have to say about all this?"

Fay flushed. "I didn't tell her. You see, all these things happened when I was alone in the house. Mother seemed to be so happy. She'd found a job that paid well. For the first time, she could see all her dreams for me coming true. She often said that perhaps the old house wasn't as bright and cheerful as it could be, but. . . ."

Trixie thought again of the old mansion as it had looked last night, and she couldn't help thinking that Mrs. Franklin's remark had been the understatement of the year.

"And so I didn't tell her," Fay continued. "I began to wonder if everything that was going on was all my imagination. I began listening to stories—gossip, really—about Lisgard House. The more I heard, the more uneasy I got. And—and then I began to wonder if I was doing all these things myself." She flung her head back and gazed at the circle of faces around her. Her eyes filled with tears. "And then one day Zeke Collins told me the story of poor Sarah Sligo. What he didn't tell me, I found out from other people. I found out that the house brings bad luck to everyone who lives there. I found out that its occupants are—well, cursed. I began to have dreams—nightmares—and Sarah would be in them. She was always dressed the same." Fay's voice was so low now that the Bob-Whites had to strain their ears to hear her. "I would be sitting in the study, the little room where she died. Suddenly the door would open, and there she'd be. 'I need you, Fay,' she'd say. 'Only you can help me. You must help me get my revenge.'"

Trixie stirred uneasily. "Those were only dreams, Fay," she said.

Fay shook her dark head. "But they were so vivid. And then, last night, Trixie told me the real story, the true story of Sarah Sligo. She didn't want to at first, but I made her. I had to know the truth about Sarah Sligo."

Trixie gasped and remembered her own hunch that she was about to make a terrible mistake if she repeated the legend of the Lisgard witch. Why hadn't she listened to her own warning?

"Oh, Fay," Trixie whispered, "I shouldn't have said anything. . . ."

Fay didn't seem to have heard her. "And so I learned the terrible truth. Somehow, someway, Sarah Sligo has taken over. How else can you explain what happened last night? Did you hear, all of you, how I almost burned us alive? *I* did it. I *must* have done it! There's no other explanation! We were asleep. I was dreaming again about Sarah. And when I woke up—" her voice broke— "the room was full of smoke."

"That's silly, Fay," Honey said sharply. "How do you account, then, for all those other sounds we heard—the axes hacking at the front door; the footsteps in the passage; the screaming?" She stopped, shuddering.

Fay leaped to her feet, her hands clenched at her sides. "I can summon the powers of darkness!" she cried. "When I am Sarah, I can do anything— anything at all!" She looked away and broke into a storm of weeping.

The Bob-Whites sat in stunned silence. Then the girls hurried to comfort her.

"Listen, Fay," sensible Honey said earnestly, "what *I* think is that you've been brooding about this for far too long. Things can't possibly have happened the way you think. It just doesn't make sense."

"It does too make sense," Fay insisted. She sniffled, then added uncertainly, "Why doesn't it make sense?"

Honey obviously had no answer to this and threw Trixie a silent appeal for help.

"It doesn't make sense," Trixie said, trying desperately to think of something, "because— because—" Suddenly she stopped. "Because I've had an idea all along that someone else was there in the house with us last night."

"The whispering witch?" asked Di.

Puzzled, Trixie ran a hand through her curls and frowned. "No," she said at last, "someone else."

Fay lifted a tearstained face from Honey's shoulder and stared. "But we were alone in the house last night. You know we were. There wasn't anyone else but us. We checked, remember?"

"I know," Trixie said obstinately, "but all the same, I'm sure I'm right. I saw something—heard something— Oh, what *was* it?"

"Maybe you'll think of it later, Trix," Brian's deep voice remarked. He turned toward Fay. "Come on, kiddo. Leave everything to Uncle Brian. It seems to me that Honey's right. You've been worrying about this ghost stuff way too much. It isn't good to do that, you know. I'm sure you're no more possessed than I am. It's time to go to visit your mother. That's going to make you feel a whole lot better." He led Fay toward the clubhouse door. "You coming, Trix?"

"I'd like to come, too, if Fay doesn't mind," Honey said.

"And me?" Di asked. "Me, too?"

In the end, it was decided that all the Bob-Whites, with the exception of Dan, would accompany Fay to the hospital.

Dan thrust his hands deep into the pockets of his corduroys. "You know I'd be with you if I could," he told Fay awkwardly, "but I guess I'd better get back to work on the game preserve."

Dan worked for Mr. Maypenny, the Wheelers' gamekeeper, and was now a well-adjusted person. There had been a time when he had been involved with a New York City street gang and had gotten into trouble with the law. Those days were long since over with, though. Now Dan's ambition was to be a policeman.

"We understand, Dan," Trixie told him, and she smiled as she watched him stride away.

She was still thinking about Fay's strange story as she and her friends climbed into the station wagon, which had been given to the Bob-Whites by Honey's father.

"If only I could remember what it was that's made me suspicious about what went on last night," Trixie whispered to Mart, who was sitting beside her in the backseat. "I know it's really important." She hesitated. "Mart, did you believe the stuff Fay told us? Do you really think she's possessed? Are there such things as ghosts? Can they come back to haunt the living? Do you—do you think Fay's telling us the truth?"

For a moment, she thought her brother wasn't going to answer her. He seemed to be busy watching Jim climb into the driver's seat.

Mart didn't say anything until the big car was heading west along Glen Road and had sped past

Lisgard House. Then he stirred and asked, "Has it occurred to you, Trix, that if Fay is telling the truth—and I did say *if*—that trying to get rid of a spirit could be very difficult?"

Trixie nodded. "Yes," she said, keeping her voice low, "I'd thought of that. In fact, I have no idea how it's done."

"You call in an exorcist," Mart said, "and sometimes they're very expensive."

Trixie stared at him, her eyes wide. "How expensive is one?"

Mart leaned his blond head closer to hers. "I don't really know," he whispered, "but I do know what happens if you don't *pay* your exorcist."

"What?"

"You get repossessed," Mart answered and laughed when he saw the look of outrage on his sister's face.

"How could you, Mart!" she hissed. "What's the matter with you, anyway? Don't you realize there's nothing funny about this? Have you *really* thought about what we're going to do if Fay's truly possessed?"

Mart looked penitent at once. "I'm sorry, Trix," he said. "It was a dumb joke, and I do know that Fay needs help. Whether the Bob-Whites can give it to her, though, is another matter. Brian seems to think she may need professional help—in other words, she may need a psychiatrist."

Trixie was silent as she stared out the window at the flying landscape. She was more upset at Mart's words than she wanted to admit, even to herself. She respected Brian's opinion, even though she didn't always follow his advice. This time she hoped, for Fay's sake, that Brian was wrong.

She stared thoughtfully at the back of Fay's curly head as she sat sandwiched between Jim and Brian in the front seat.

Fay seemed to feel that someone was watching her, because she twisted around, smiled at Trixie, and said, "I feel a lot better now. It seems to help when you can share troubles with your friends. There's just one more thing, though."

Trixie groaned inwardly. What terrible thing was Fay going to tell them now?

"I'd appreciate it," Fay continued shyly, "if you didn't tell my mother what we've been talking about. It would worry her very much."

"Of course we won't tell her, Fay," Honey said at once. "In fact, we won't tell anyone."

The big car nosed its way into the hospital parking lot and backed into a space.

"Oh, Fay!" Trixie exclaimed suddenly. "What did you say about not telling anyone? Something tells me that's not going to be as easy as you think, but I certainly hope I'm wrong!"

Startled, Fay turned to look out of the front-seat window. "What do you mean, Trixie?" Then she stopped, appalled.

She found herself staring at a group of people who were already hurrying toward her. One woman carried a portable television camera on her shoulder. Her partner, a young man with flashing white teeth and dimples in his cheeks, was already thrusting a microphone toward Fay's frightened face. A scruffy-looking young man had positioned himself with his still camera, ready to take a photograph, while Paul Trent, a newspaper reporter for the *Sleepyside Sun*, scribbled furiously in his notebook.

"Hold on a minute there, Miss Franklin," Mr. Teeth-and-Dimples was saying. "How would you like to tell your exciting story to our television viewers on the five-thirty news tonight?"

Fay looked bewildered. "What—what exciting story?"

Paul Trent thrust his head through the open window and peered curiously into her face. "We want you to tell us all about the curious haunting of Lisgard House, of course," he said. "We got a tip that the witch tried to burn the place down last night. You might just as well give us the straight dope, you know. We've already heard a lot about it. C'mon girls, give us the whole story."

Fay stiffened, then turned her head to look behind her. Her eyes were filled with tears. "Oh, Trixie," she whispered. "How could you!"

Mashed Potatoes · 10

FIVE MINUTES LATER, Trixie was still protesting her innocence as she and her friends hurried through the hospital's main entrance. She could tell by the way Fay wouldn't quite catch her eye, though, that she didn't believe her.

Fay had flatly refused to talk to either the newspaper reporter or his television counterpart. "Please! I don't want to talk to you!" she kept repeating over and over in answer to their persistent questions.

In the end, it was Brian and Jim who put a stop to all further argument by taking her by the arms and rushing her firmly away.

"Jeepers!" Mart exclaimed once they were in the hospital lobby. "I feel as if I've been run over by a truck!"

"I know. I do, too," Honey admitted, brushing her long golden hair out of her eyes. "Did you hear all the questions they asked?"

"I heard," Di put in. " 'What did the ghost look like?' 'What did she say?' 'How did you get out of there alive?' "

Fay started toward the large reception desk, but Trixie had planted herself firmly in her path. "Listen," Trixie said earnestly, "I don't know who told those reporters about last night, Fay, but it wasn't me, honestly! Why would I do such a thing?"

Fay still looked upset. "I don't know," she answered. "But those reporters said they'd had an anonymous tip. On the phone, they said. I know it couldn't have been Honey. She and I were together all night and again this morning."

"I was with you, too," Trixie protested.

"Not after breakfast," Fay said, her voice low. "Honey and I left you talking with your brothers, if you'll remember. You could have used the telephone then—that is, unless it was—" She stopped and stared thoughtfully at Brian and Mart.

"Hey, back off!" Mart said, throwing up his hands in a show of mock horror. "We weren't the anonymous tipper-offers, either."

"Well, then—" Fay looked bewildered. "If it wasn't Trixie, and if it wasn't Brian or Mart, then who could it have been? Who else knew about it? The reporters said the call came in early this morning. No one else knew about it then." She smiled at Jim and Di. "Even you hadn't heard the story."

"Not that early," Jim said, running his hand perplexedly through his red hair. "Anyone got any ideas?"

But not one had.

Trixie was still thinking about it when Fay returned from the information desk with the number of her mother's room.

Trixie heard Honey say, "Why don't you go visit your mother alone, Fay? The rest of us don't mind waiting out here."

"That's right," Trixie said absently. "Anyway, we can go see a couple of friends in the gift shop. Honey and I work as Volunteens here in the summer sometimes, and—" She broke off.

"And what?" Brian demanded.

"Hold on to your hats!" Mart exclaimed. "Ms. Sherlock Belden has got one of those a-thought-has-just-struck-me looks on her face."

"It was the door," Trixie breathed.

Jim frowned and glanced over his shoulder.

"What door are you talking about, Trixie?"

"The back door at Lisgard House," Trixie replied impatiently. "I've been trying and trying to remember what made me think someone else could have been there last night. It was the back door. I'm sure of it. I heard it close."

"Or open?" Brian asked.

Trixie shook her head. "I don't think so. It was after those terrible noises we heard, and after the room was filled with smoke. Just as we were sure we were all going to die, the noises stopped. The smoke began to clear. But why? How could it? Fay's bedroom didn't have any window."

"Maybe it was more black magic," Honey began, then looked as if she wished she hadn't. "Er—that is, what I meant was—"

Trixie wasn't listening. "I opened the bedroom door. The passage outside was cold—very cold, as if cold air had been blowing through it. It was then I heard a door close—the back door. Oh, don't you see? It's the only solution. Someone else must have been there! *But who?*"

"If you're right," Mart said slowly, "then undoubtedly the dirty-deed-doer was the anonymous informant as far as the boob-tube people were concerned. She must have called good ol' Paul Trent at the same time."

"She?" Honey said, looking puzzled.

125

"A slip of the protrusible oral organ," Mart said loftily, "in other words, tongue, Trix. I could as easily have figured the stool pigeon as male."

All the same, Trixie noticed that Mart didn't look at Fay. *So he still suspects her of playing some game of her own*, she thought.

After Fay had hurried away, the Bob-Whites discussed Trixie's theory about the possible identity of the intruder—if, indeed, there had been one, which Mart seemed to doubt.

As no one had anything helpful to add, however, it wasn't long before the girls hurried away to the gift shop, while the boys flung themselves into the lobby's chairs to wait.

Trixie was busy talking to Mariellen Hanrahan, the only Volunteen on duty behind the counter that day, when a voice said in her ear, "So this is where you've got to. I've been looking all over for you, Trixie."

Trixie swung around and found herself looking into the kindly face of Dr. Ferris. "How's Mrs. Franklin?" she asked, smiling at him.

"Doing well," he answered. "You've heard, of course, that we've got to keep her here at the hospital for several more days. But by the time we're finished with her, she'll be as good as new—you'll see. Now, about that daughter of hers: Brian tells me you've invited her to stay at

Crabapple Farm. Then see that you fatten her up. That child is much too skinny—not at all like the bouncing Beldens, eh?" He chuckled at his own mild joke as Trixie reddened. Then he glanced at Honey and Di, who had gathered close to hear his news. "Of course, young Fay would do just as well if she stayed with the lovable Lynches or the wonderful Wheelers."

Obediently, the girls laughed.

"We're glad that Mrs. Franklin is going to be okay," Honey told him. "Fay was very worried about her."

Dr. Ferris looked down at her. "Those two worry about each other too much," he said. "I think, too, that Mrs. Franklin is anxious to get back to her job. She seems to think she's going to lose it if she takes time off. I asked her what was more important—her health or her work. And bless me if she didn't have to stop and think about it. Why anyone would want to stay at Lisgard House is more than I can understand. Ah, well, it takes all kinds to make a world."

"I think the Franklins need the money," Di put in. "Mr. Gregory pays a good salary."

Dr. Ferris nodded his head. "So that explains it. I wondered, y'know. The last time I was there, I thought the place looked like a morgue—or a museum."

Trixie's mind snapped suddenly to attention. "The last time you were there? Was that when old Mr. Lisgard died?"

Dr. Ferris nodded. "Yes, it was. Poor old fellow. I expect you heard. I got there too late. Couldn't do a thing for him. Of course, I'd warned him it was going to happen."

"Warned him that what was going to happen?" Trixie asked, thinking of the story Regan had told her. "Did he really see the witch and then have a heart attack and die of shock?"

Dr. Ferris stared. "Now, where did you hear a story like that?" he asked sharply. "That's the most ridiculous nonsense I've ever heard."

"You mean it isn't true?" Trixie said slowly.

"Of course it isn't true! Not a word of it! If you must know, young lady, old Mr. Lisgard had suffered from high blood pressure for years. I warned him that he mustn't have any excitement at all, but he didn't listen. One night he lost his temper with his housekeeper. She upped and stormed out of there, never to return. Caleb promptly had a stroke and died. Take my word for it!"

"Then he didn't have a heart attack?" Trixie asked.

Dr. Ferris stared at her sternly. "He died of a stroke brought on by a bowl of mashed potatoes, if you must know. I made it my business to find out all the strange details afterward."

"He died of a bowl of *what?*" Honey gasped.

"Mashed potatoes," Dr. Ferris repeated. "He'd ordered 'em baked, you see. His housekeeper forgot and mashed 'em, instead. He lost his temper over it, and there you are! You can tell everyone I said so, too. Died of a witch's ghost—or the sight of one? I never heard of such a thing!"

Trixie was tempted to tell him that she'd never before heard of anyone dying of a bowl of mashed potatoes, either, but thought better of it.

Dr. Ferris turned to leave. "How's that young nephew-in-law of Caleb's getting on?" he asked. "I expect he's tidied up the place quite a bit now, with Zeke's help. Repainted it, I have no doubt, and made it look a lot more cheerful. Apart from that antique furniture of his, old Caleb had no taste when it came to decorating his house."

"No," Honey told him, "Mr. Gregory hasn't repainted anything—at least, it doesn't look like it. Trixie and I were there last night—"

Dr. Ferris shook his head. "Ah, well, maybe the young man's a chip off the Lisgard block—though I don't quite see how that could be, considering young Lewis Gregory's only an in-law. I must say, I felt very sorry for that young man when he took over that big old run-down house. People around here tell me he was raised in the city, so I daresay he'd rather be back there than stuck way out here in Sleepyside."

"I can't see how anyone can prefer living anywhere else but here," Honey remarked.

"Ah, but then your family also has money to enjoy it with, young lady," Dr. Ferris answered, smiling at her. "You see, old Caleb didn't have any money to leave young Lewis—at least, not nearly as much as everyone thought."

"I always thought old Mr. Lisgard was rich," Trixie said thoughtfully.

"Everyone did." Dr. Ferris sighed. "But in the last months of his life, Caleb made some pretty bad investments—a lot of them. Result? Money gone. So there you are. Young Mr. Gregory inherited a white elephant of a house and no money to run it with. Yes, I feel sorry for that young man. Ah, well, there's nothing I can do about it. I must be off. Be sure and fatten up the Franklin girl while she's staying with you, Trixie."

He strode out of the gift shop and was gone.

Honey stared after him, obviously still thinking about what he'd told them. "Trixie, who told you that Mr. Lisgard died of shock from seeing the witch's ghost?" she asked.

Trixie giggled and led the way out of the shop and back to the boys. "Regan told me," she said. "I can't wait to tell him the true story!"

The Psychic Medium • 11

ALL THE WAY HOME in the car, Trixie was thinking about everything that had happened since Fay had come pounding on the Beldens' door the previous evening. So much had occurred in that short time. So much still had to be explained.

She glanced at Fay out of the corner of her eye and wondered what she was thinking. Did she still believe that she was possessed by the witch's spirit? Did she really believe that she could summon the powers of darkness at will?

When the Bob-Whites had looked briefly into Mrs. Franklin's room before leaving the hospital, it was obvious that Fay had told her mother nothing of their frightening experiences the night before.

Mrs. Franklin had looked relaxed and had been obviously glad to see them. She had once more thanked them warmly for looking after her daughter—and no mention had been made of any witch, or ghost, or rooms filled with smoke.

Now Trixie wondered if Fay had been wise to keep this information from her mother. If the press was already hot on the trail of this kind of story, it was likely that Mrs. Franklin would soon discover what had happened in her absence.

"Maybe you should have told her," Trixie said to Fay, who was seated beside her on this return trip.

Fay jumped, as if her thoughts had been a million miles away. Then, when Trixie explained, she smiled and said, "I've already made sure the newspaper people won't bother Mother—or the television crew, either. I spoke to Dr. Ferris about it. Don't worry. Mother won't even see a paper or a television set for a while."

Honey had been listening from the front seat. She turned her head and remarked over her shoulder, "All the same, Fay, it might not have been a bad idea to tell your mother something about it. It's going to come as a terrific shock once she finds out."

But Fay only shook her head and repeated that she didn't want her mother worried right now. Trixie dropped the subject, sensing that Fay didn't want to discuss it any further.

Jim slowed the big car as it neared the grounds of Lisgard House. "Do I use the back entrance, Fay?" he asked.

Fay frowned, puzzled. "Why are you stopping, Jim?" she asked.

Brian glanced at her. "Didn't we hear something about picking up some clothes?"

"*I* heard that some bubble-headed females packed bathing suits last night," Mart observed.

Trixie was startled when she heard Fay laugh aloud. It was as if her spirits had suddenly lightened, and her fears, if not quite gone, were at least held in check for a while.

"If you wouldn't mind, all of you," Fay said, "I really would prefer to leave it till later. I need to see Mr. Gregory, you see, and he won't be home till sometime this afternoon. I need to tell him about Mother's accident—and she wants me to tell him she'll be back at work as soon as she can."

"Jeepers!" Mart exclaimed. "What an admirable devotion to duty."

"Of course, you can do whatever you want, Fay," Brian said, "but if you're feeling nervous about going in there alone, maybe you'd better leave it till later on tonight."

"Why does she have to leave it?" Trixie demanded. "You've already promised me you'd come with us."

"We thought you meant now," Mart explained. "I mean, after we'd been to the hospital. The thing is, Trix, that Brian, Jim, and I have a date."

Trixie stared. "What kind of date?"

"It is an engagement with a comely damsel who is demure of eye and fair of face," Mart replied. "She is to be relentlessly pursued by a bashful swain who is too solemnly silent to be believed."

Trixie glared at him. "Oh, for crying out loud, Mart! What are you talking about?"

"I'm afraid he means that we've been booked for the school's Thanksgiving play," Brian said, "and rehearsals start this afternoon. Jim is playing the part of Miles Standish, I'm going to be bashful John, and one of Mart's classmates—"

"A female," Mart added needlessly.

"—is playing the part of Priscilla."

"And I'm the stage manager," Mart finished. "And so, you see, irate sibling, our services have been engaged by the Sleepyside Junior-Senior High School for this afternoon. Either we accompany you to Lisgard House right now—"

"—or I'm afraid you're going to have to go there by yourselves this afternoon," Jim said, looking sorry about the turn of events.

Trixie could tell that Fay and Honey felt as unhappy as she did about the way things had worked out.

"I'll come with you," Di said suddenly, pushing the dark, shining curtain of hair away from her pretty face. "Fay needs clothes; she also needs to see Mr. Gregory, who isn't home yet; and I wouldn't miss seeing inside that house for the world. Besides, it's daylight. Whoever heard of a ghost appearing in the afternoon? Okay, girls?"

Slowly and reluctantly, the girls nodded their assent.

"It'll be fine," Trixie told Fay reassuringly as the big car sped homeward toward the safety of Crabapple Farm. But as they turned into the Beldens' graveled driveway, she discovered that she was crossing all of her fingers.

It wasn't long after this that Trixie, remembering her promise to Regan, suggested that they should take the horses on their trip back to Fay's new home. At two o'clock, the four girls met in the Wheelers' stable yard.

Di, mounted on Sunny, her palomino, watched patiently as Trixie and Honey saddled Lady, Susie, and Strawberry.

Trixie had already whispered in Starlight's ear that he would get his turn another time, because the other Bob-Whites were busy and there was no one left to ride him.

Starlight had nodded his head almost as if he understood and forgave them all.

When the girls were nearly finished with getting their mounts ready, they heard Regan's voice call, "Don't forget to tighten Lady's cinch." He appeared from around the side of the stable and strode toward them. Soon he was running an experienced hand over the leather cinch that Honey had just tightened.

Trixie grinned at him. Ever since she had known him, Regan had never failed to mention that Lady had a habit of "blowing herself up" when she was being saddled. Her cinch had to be tightened after riding a short distance; otherwise the saddle loosened and slipped.

Only once had Trixie forgotten. But Regan hadn't. He had not enjoyed watching her being tumbled helplessly from the dapple gray mare's back onto the hard ground below. On that occasion, it had taken repeated assurances to convince him that she wasn't hurt. He didn't intend to let it happen again.

"Don't worry, Regan," Trixie told him now. "We've already asked Fay, and she's quite used to horses. In fact, she's quite an accomplished horse-woman. She was just telling us about it."

"My mother had a job on a ranch one time," Fay explained shyly. "The school I attended was pretty far away, so the only way I could get there was on horseback. Mr. Larson, the ranch owner, helped me. He taught me to ride and lent me a horse, too." She sighed. "I still miss old Smoky."

Trixie glanced at her with sympathy. *It must be awful never having a home or a pet of your own,* she thought. *I wonder how many homes Fay has had? How many has she had to leave when she really didn't want to?*

Regan watched as Fay lifted herself into Strawberry's saddle, while Trixie mounted Susie.

"We won't be too long, Regan," promised Honey, who already sat astride the mischievous Lady. "And I *will* remember to tighten the cinch again."

"And we *won't* take the horses for a fast gallop through the woods," Trixie added, grinning down at Regan's worried face.

"To say nothing of jumping fallen trees," Di couldn't resist saying.

For a moment, Trixie thought they'd gone too far, for Regan was frowning up at them.

At last, obviously realizing they were only teasing, he said, "Well, you just be careful."

The other girls had already moved out of the stable yard. Trixie was about to join them, when Regan put a restraining hand on Susie's bridle.

"One more thing, Trixie," Regan said. "If you see Zeke, don't you let him scare you with one of his weird tales."

Trixie was startled. She'd forgotten all about the Lisgard odd-job man. Now she thought of the stains on his overalls. Had they been blood?

"Does he like to hunt?" she asked Regan abruptly.

"Who, Zeke?" Regan scratched his red head. "Not that I know of. Why?"

Trixie told him of Zeke's strange appearance and was surprised when Regan laughed. "I expect it was just paint," he said. "Zeke's been doing a lot of painting lately."

"Oh!" Trixie's face fell and she felt a pang of disappointment upon hearing such a mundane explanation of the stains.

She turned Susie's head toward the three girls, who were waiting for her. At the last moment, however, she couldn't resist leaning from her saddle and whispering to Regan, "I found out what Caleb Lisgard died of. It was a bowl of mashed potatoes." She laughed when she noticed the puzzled look in his face.

The four girls were riding easily when they came in sight of Lisgard House.

Suddenly Fay gasped and pulled Strawberry to a halt as she stared straight ahead of her.

Startled, Trixie raised herself in her saddle to get a better look and found herself gazing at a small group of people gathered outside the mansion's iron front gates.

She recognized four of them at once. They were the same members of the press who had tried to get Fay to talk to them at the hospital parking lot. There were, however, two additions to the group. One, Trixie knew, was Lewis Gregory, the owner of Lisgard House. A dark-haired young man, he seemed to have no hesitation in talking earnestly to the reporters.

Trixie had never seen the other man before. He stood quietly. His long, thin face wore a serious and intent expression. A long cape hung from his shoulders. It made him look, she thought, a little like a magician about to pull a rabbit from a hat.

Trixie heard Mr. Gregory announce, "And so, you see, I've been aware all along of the strange things that have been happening in my house. Is the place haunted? Has Sarah Sligo been summoned from her grave to exact her revenge on the innocent citizens of Sleepyside? Is there any truth to the persistent rumors that the witch's phantom inhabits my property?"

"Yeah?" Paul Trent prompted him, his pencil

poised. "And what's the answer?"

"That," Mr. Gregory said, "is what we're about to find out. Folks, I want you to meet someone. This man"—he gestured toward the silent stranger—"is none other than Mr. Simon Hunter, the famous psychic investigator."

"Jeepers!" Trixie muttered under her breath. "I've never met one of those before. I wonder what a psychic investigator does?"

Honey leaned sideways in her saddle and then whispered in her ear, "I've heard they're sort of like ghost detectives. They investigate psychic phenomena."

They watched as the man in the black cape stirred but said nothing.

"And so I've invited Mr. Hunter to come and discover exactly what's going on at Lisgard House," Mr. Gregory said.

"Is this true?" the television reporter asked. At last Trixie remembered his name. It was Ed Gaffey, from Sleepyside's small television station. The Beldens seldom watched him.

Mr. Hunter smiled. "It's quite true," he replied quietly. "There are many stories of hauntings in our country. Some prove to be merely rumor and gossip. Some are not."

Paul Trent scratched his head with the end of his pencil. "And the haunting of Lisgard House?

Which do you think this is? Do you think it's possible for someone around here to be dabbling in black magic? Can a person call a dead spirit from the grave?"

Mr. Hunter hesitated. "It's not only possible," he said at last, "but from what I've been told about this case so far, I'd say it's very likely."

Ed Gaffey frowned. "Then who is it who's doing all this witchcraft-black-magic stuff? Do you have any ideas?"

"I have lots of ideas," Mr. Hunter answered grimly, "though not necessarily the correct ones— not yet, anyway."

Trixie leaned forward and strained her ears to hear.

"You see," Mr. Hunter continued, "the person who's calling Sarah Sligo from her grave may not be aware that she—or he—is doing so. On the other hand, she might be doing it deliberately."

And Trixie saw him lift his head and gaze straight into the terrified eyes of Fay Franklin.

A Ghostly Presence · 12

I TELL YOU HE KNOWS!" Fay said for the third time. "You must have seen him. He looked straight at me and said *someone* was calling the witch from her grave. And it *is* me. I'm sure of it now!"

The four girls stood in Fay's bedroom, where they had arrived only moments before. The horses had been tethered close to the mansion's back gate and were, Trixie imagined, munching contentedly on a nearby evergreen shrub. She only hoped it wasn't a prize one.

Di's violet eyes opened wide as she stared around the room. "Is this where it all happened last night?" she asked.

Fay didn't seem to have heard her. "I was beginning to think I'd been imagining everything," Fay continued. "I—I was beginning to forget. Being away from this house helped a lot. But now that I'm back, I can feel Sarah Sligo's presence around me."

Trixie felt worried, and she could tell that Honey and Di were as concerned as she was. It still wasn't clear whether or not Fay was fooling them all. But Trixie was beginning to think that her agitation was quite genuine.

"Come on, Fay," Honey said suddenly. "This place is enough to give anyone the creeps. Let's grab your clothes and get out of here. You'll feel better once we get you away from here again."

Trixie knew that Honey was right. All the same, she couldn't help feeling a pang of disappointment. If they left now, she'd never be able to discover exactly what a ghost detective did in order to track down his phantom prey.

She was trying to think of an excuse that would allow her three friends to leave while she stayed behind to watch, when Fay shuddered.

"I won't ever feel better until Mother and I are away from here for good," she whispered. "I can see that now. I thought I could stand it, for Mother's sake, but I can't! I don't ever want to come here again!"

"But then, my dear," a smooth voice said from the doorway, "you wouldn't ever be able to rest again. Running away from a problem doesn't help, you know. You'll be worried about it for the rest of your life." It was Mr. Hunter.

Fay took a step toward him. "What—what do you mean?"

Mr. Hunter stepped into the room and gazed at her intently. "I would like you to stay here for a while today," he said. "I want you to tell me everything you know about what's been happening. Don't be afraid. I won't let the psychic forces attack. You'll be quite safe."

"No!" There was a note of panic in Fay's voice. "Things have been getting worse," she cried. "Something is going on that I don't understand. If I'm the one who's calling Sarah from her grave, I haven't—I didn't—" She stopped, her hand over her mouth, watching Mr. Hunter with frightened eyes.

He nodded slowly and sat down on the tumble of blankets on the armchair that had been Trixie's bed the night before. He looked around the room. "So that's it," he said quietly. "I expected as much. I wasn't sure, you see, where Sarah was getting her energy from."

Trixie stared. "I don't think we understand. Are you saying that it's *Fay* who's been causing all the

144

spooky happenings around here?"

Mr. Hunter made a steeple out of his long, thin fingers and tapped them thoughtfully against his mouth. "Let's just say this," he continued at last. "It *could* have been your friend's psychic energy that has attracted Sarah Sligo's spirit. Mind, I'm not saying definitely yet that it was. I'm saying it *could* have been. Spirits who are in—" he hesitated— "in the other world often need a channel to allow them to return to this plane. Those channels often lend themselves willingly to a disembodied entity."

"And when that happens, are these channels called mediums?" Honey asked eagerly.

Mr. Hunter nodded. "They are indeed, my child. Then there are other channels—unwitting ones, perhaps." He looked thoughtfully at Fay. "Sometimes the unwitting channel attracts spirits who are evil. Sometimes these evil spirits cause strange events to happen. Strange rappings are heard in a house, for instance. Sometimes objects fly through the air without warning."

Trixie frowned. "Are you talking about polter —polter—oh, what's the name of them?"

"Poltergeists," Mr. Hunter told her. "But I don't believe we're dealing with a poltergeist at Lisgard House. What we're talking about is an entity who is seeking revenge. She cannot rest, you see. And to return to the scene of her death, she had to wait until she found the correct channel—the one person who could provide her with enough psychic energy to bring her to this plane from that other world we call death."

"And whom did she find?" Di asked, her eyes wide.

"I suspect she found our young friend here," Mr. Hunter said softly. "It is well known that spirits often search until they find a teen-ager. How old are you, Fay?" His voice was gentle.

"Fourteen," Fay whispered and collapsed onto the side of her bed as if her legs would no longer hold her.

"Yes," Mr. Hunter said, nodding his head. "That is a good age for our spirit friends. A child of fourteen or, let's say, the teen-age years, is in a period of tremendous growth both physically and mentally. Now, why don't you tell me what's been happening here in the last few months?"

"Good idea," a voice said from the doorway, and they turned to see Mr. Gregory smiling at them. "I'd like to hear this story, too. Some of it I've already heard from your mother, Fay."

Fay looked startled. *"Mother?* Mother knows what's been going on?"

"Of course." Mr. Gregory looked surprised. "Do you mean to tell me the two of you haven't discussed this between yourselves? Ah!" He clapped a hand to his head. "I forgot! Your mother didn't want you to know. She had an idea that things happened only when she was here alone." He smiled. "Don't be afraid, Fay. Nothing can hurt you now. Let's discuss this in another room—the living room, perhaps."

As if in a dream, Fay and her friends followed the two men until they were seated, if not comfortably, then at least spaciously, in the large room with its gloomy, massive furniture.

Mr. Gregory began by saying that he'd learned of his housekeeper's accident from Dr. Ferris only a short time before. He sounded concerned and said he would call the hospital as soon as his telephone was fixed.

Then he and Mr. Hunter listened quietly as Fay repeated the story she had already told the Bob-Whites.

Fay told them everything—even about Trixie's fright over the "mouse." Trixie didn't correct her. For some strange reason, she decided not to mention the scary figure she'd seen in the kitchen hall. She still needed time to think quietly about this by herself.

She supposed the ghost detective really knew what he was talking about. All the same, the information he'd given them was incredible. She wondered what her brothers would say about it when she told them.

Soon Fay was at that point in her story where Trixie and Honey could confirm the previous night's strange events.

Mr. Hunter's face grew stern and grim as he listened. At last he stirred, his fingers formed another steeple, and he leaned back in his wing chair by the empty, blackened fireplace and closed his eyes.

"And you say you thought you heard the back door close?" he asked suddenly. He opened his eyes and directed a penetrating stare at Trixie.

From her seat on the couch, Trixie gazed back at him and nodded firmly. "Yes," she said. "The more I think about it, the more certain I am."

"Couldn't have been what you thought it was," Mr. Hunter said suddenly. "What I mean is, it couldn't have been through any *human* agency. That door must have been closed by Sarah. There's no doubt about it. This is a fine example of what we were talking about before. Spirits often open and close doors—"

"That's true, Trixie," Fay interrupted eagerly. "I often heard them doing that when I was here by myself. I'm not sure I mentioned that before."

Mr. Hunter got to his feet and stroked his chin. "I think you've called me in just in time, Lew," he said grimly. "It's quite obvious what's happening. Things are getting worse. I don't yet know why. But I'll find out—oh, yes, I'll find out before I'm through."

He began prowling around the room, stopping every so often to lift his head as if he was listening to sounds—or voices—that only he could hear.

"What is it?" Di asked. "What's he doing?"

Mr. Gregory, seated on the other side of the fireplace, put a finger against his lips. "Hush, my dear," he said softly. "Mr. Hunter is not only a psychic investigator, but he's also a medium himself. He communicates with the spirit world. And he's promised me he'll try to get in touch with Sarah's spirit, in order to try to turn her away from her evil purposes—whatever they may be."

Trixie was fascinated. "Now?" she couldn't resist asking. "Is he going to do it now?"

Honey gripped her arm, warning her to be quiet, then watched as Mr. Hunter turned, as if irresistibly drawn, to the doorway leading to that small study where the witch had died so many years before.

Trixie heard Fay gasp as, with a sudden movement that startled his watchers, Mr. Hunter flung open the study door.

She was entirely unprepared for the strange,

startling events that happened next.

A blast of cold air rushed toward them. It brushed their staring faces with icy fingers. A tall vase on the mantlepiece swayed, then crashed to the floor and smashed into fragments. The thin drapes at the tall windows bellied inward toward the room's startled occupants.

Mr. Hunter flung back his head, threw his arms wide, as if in welcome, and cried, "Sarah Sligo, if this is your spirit, I command you to tell me. Speak!"

At once, all movement stopped. Then, in the stillness, someone laughed.

The Eavesdropper · 13

THE GIRLS SAT, as if frozen, until that terrible laughter died away. Then there was silence.

Mr. Hunter turned toward his stunned audience. "It's all right," he said. "Please don't be afraid. I had to find out, you see. I needed to know if the vengeful spirit really was Sarah's ghost. And now we know."

Mr. Gregory looked shaken as he got to his feet. "And is it?"

Trixie wasn't surprised when Mr. Hunter answered grimly, "It is. And now all we have to do is to find out how to get rid of her."

"But can you do that?" Trixie burst out. "Is it

possible to exorcise someone who's been dead for years and years?"

For a moment, the psychic investigator didn't answer. Then he looked at Fay and said gently, "That depends on how much our young friend here is willing to help."

Fay sat pale and shaken. She stared down at her hands, which were clasped tightly in her lap. "Yes," she said at last, "I'll help you. I—I can't live with this fear anymore." She looked at Trixie. "I don't want to be a channel for a spirit. I've got to get rid of Sarah once and for all."

Honey looked as shaken as Fay. Trixie guessed that the past few minutes had frightened her a great deal. She was glad to see, though, that Honey was doing her best to hide her feelings.

"We understand," Honey told Fay, leaning forward to pat her hand, "and if you need any help, we'll be right here with you."

"Sure we will," Trixie added warmly and waited for Di to add her assurances to theirs.

To her surprise, Di said nothing. Then, when Trixie turned her head to look, she noticed that Di wasn't even there. She had moved quietly to the study door and was gazing curiously around the little room.

"Di?" Trixie called.

Di had already taken several steps into the

study, but now she retreated hastily. "I just had to see where the witch died," she confessed. "I'm sorry. I was listening, though, honestly. And of course I'll help you, Fay." She smiled. "You'll soon learn that our motto is 'all for one and one for all.' Well, if it isn't, it should be."

Mr. Hunter looked pleased, as if things were working out the way he'd hoped. He rubbed his hands together. "Thank you, girls," he said. "You won't regret this, I'm sure. And now that we have this settled, all I need to know now is exactly what the circumstances were surrounding our entity's death."

Trixie was startled. "You mean you don't know?"

Mr. Hunter settled himself back into his chair. "I know what Lew Gregory has told me," he said, "but perhaps it would be as well if I heard yet another version from someone who's lived here for a long time."

"That's Trixie," Honey said, still looking as if she wished they could leave.

Trixie repeated the story of Sarah Sligo, while once more her audience listened quietly.

When she had finished, Mr. Hunter stirred in his seat. "And you say she was burned to death on Thanksgiving night?" he asked.

Trixie nodded. "Yes."

"And she was also born on Thanksgiving day

thirty-four years before that," Fay put in suddenly.

Trixie stared. "She was? Why, I didn't know that! Who told you? I thought no one knew the exact day she was born. Her grave was never found."

"Her grave is here on the grounds of Lisgard House," Fay said, her voice low. "I'll show you later, if you like. I—I was interested, you see, and when Zeke Collins offered to show me where she was buried. . . ."

Trixie, Honey, and Di exchanged startled glances over the top of Fay's bent head.

Trixie in particular was astonished. She'd never had any inkling that Sarah's final resting place was right there at Lisgard House. She supposed someone should have suspected that it would be, long before this.

"Not only that," Fay was continuing, "but it's a well-known fact that a person who dies a violent death on the day of her birth is doomed to haunt the scene forever." She raised her head and looked at the investigator. "Is that true?"

Mr. Hunter nodded his head. "Yes, my child. It's quite true." He sighed heavily. "And that presents us with a problem I'd hoped I wouldn't have to mention." He hesitated. His steepled fingers once more tapped gently against his pursed lips. His hands dropped to his lap as if he'd come to a sudden decision. "It means that everything is now explained," he said simply. "It's the anniversary not only of her death but also of her birth. Sarah can't rest, you see, and she's becoming more and more active as that date approaches."

Trixie stared at him. "You mean something's going to happen *this* Thanksgiving night? Why— but that's next Thursday!"

Mr. Hunter sighed. "Exactly!"

It seemed to Trixie that they sat in that living room for hours, discussing what to do. Afterward, she discovered that less than an hour had passed since they'd first entered the room.

Mr. Hunter left them at last, assuring them warmly that Fay had nothing more to worry about. He said he would call them—all of them—as soon as he and Mr. Gregory were ready to exorcise Sarah's ghost and lay her forever to rest.

Trixie's thoughts were still in a whirl as she and her three friends stood in the entrance hall. She had never before experienced anything like this! Events had moved so swiftly that she felt she hadn't had time to consider any of them. It was as if they were all under some kind of enchantment —a spell from which there was no escape.

Honey smiled when Trixie told her about it. "I

know what you mean, Trix," she said. "I've been feeling the same way."

Di glanced around her and noticed the gloomy trophies that hung on the walls. Then, while Fay and Honey hurried to pack some of the needed clothes—not bathing suits this time!—Trixie showed Di the rest of the downstairs rooms.

Di was strangely silent as the four girls left the old mansion and hurried toward the back gate, where their horses waited patiently.

Trixie was about to ask her if anything was wrong, when she thought suddenly of something else. "Sarah Sligo's grave!" she exclaimed. "You promised to show us where the witch was buried, Fay."

Honey moaned. "Oh, Trix, do we have to? The more I think about it, the more I think how good it'll be to get home to Manor House."

"It'll only take a moment," Fay promised, leading them toward a tangle of undergrowth at the side of the house.

She parted a low-growing shrub with her hand and pointed. "There it is," she said. "I've been here often in the last few weeks. I wanted to cut back some of this shrubbery and make it look neat. But Zeke Collins said I was to leave it alone."

Trixie stared down at the small, white headstone. She had expected it to be indecipherable after all these years. But the words carved there were as clear as if they'd been engraved only yesterday. They said simply:

HERE LIES SARAH SLIGO
BORN THANKSGIVING DAY, 1755
DIED THANKSGIVING NIGHT, 1789

"I looked up the dates in the encyclopedia," Fay said, looking down at the grave. "Sarah died on November the twenty-sixth, Trixie. I was able to check it because that was when President Washington proclaimed the first national Thanksgiving holiday after the American Revolution."

Di had been calculating the date in her mind, Trixie thought, because she said quickly, "Then that *is* right. Today is Saturday the twenty-first—"

"And that makes next Thursday the twenty-sixth," Honey put in. "The exact date when Sarah was killed."

Fay let the bushes fall back into place and turned to face her friends. "I didn't mean for you all to get involved in the haunting of Lisgard House," she said, "but you have no idea how much you've all helped me. For one thing, I've had no one to talk to about it. I thought at one time I was going crazy. I had nowhere to turn."

Honey put her arm around Fay's thin shoulders. "Try not to worry, Fay," she said. "There's nothing you can do now, until Mr. Hunter has made his arrangements. He said he'd let us know when he was ready." She paused. "Trixie? Do you really think Sarah Sligo's getting ready to do something evil on the anniversary of her death?"

Trixie drew a deep breath. "I have a hunch that something's going to happen," she said, "and soon."

Then, out of the corner of her eye, she caught a glimpse of a sudden movement. As she watched, she saw the figure of Zeke Collins turn from the shelter of a nearby tree and hurry away toward the old mansion.

How long he'd been standing there, she had no idea. But one thing was certain: He'd been listening closely to every word they'd said.

Questionable Antiques · 14

ON THE WAY HOME, Trixie was only half listening to her friends' conversation as the horses trotted smartly along Glen Road.

She heard Fay exclaim several times over the fact that she and her mother had each been trying to protect the other.

"I had no idea that Mother knew anything was wrong at Lisgard House," Fay said.

Trixie frowned and thought again about how much Mrs. Franklin must have needed the salary her employer was paying her to stay there.

She wondered, too, how Mrs. Franklin had happened to slip and fall last night. Had it been just an accident, or had she seen—or heard—something that had startled her so much that she lost her footing?

The closer Trixie came to her home, the more unreal the events of these last few hours seemed. She let Susie's reins slacken in her hand and watched absently as her three friends rode easily in front of her.

She half heard Di remark, "Well, I think it's wonderful, Fay, that you and your mother are so concerned about each other."

"I do, too," Honey agreed, obviously thinking of her own mother, who rarely had to be worried about anything.

"What do you think, Trix?" Di called over her shoulder.

"The trouble is," Trixie said thoughtfully, "I don't really believe it."

She caught a glimpse of three startled faces turned toward her. Three pairs of hands pulled gently on their reins to allow Trixie and Susie to draw abreast of them.

"But it's true, Trixie," Fay cried, sounding hurt. "My mother and I *do* worry about each other. There's only us, you see—"

"I didn't mean that, Fay," Trixie interrupted. "I was talking about the witch's ghost. It's just—it seems—" She took a deep breath. "Oh, don't you see?" she burst out. "The whole thing's *weird*. I simply can't get over what happened last night and again this afternoon. Each time it was as if we were sort of spectators at some strange play."

"Except that I was part of it," Fay said, her voice low. "I've been a part of it all along. Oh, Trixie! You must have read about other houses, other hauntings where strange things have happened. No one's ever been able to explain them, either."

Trixie frowned and remembered the glimpse they'd had of Zeke Collins that afternoon. "I keep thinking that the odd-job man's got something to do with all this. Regan says the stains on his overalls last night were probably paint."

Honey looked surprised. "But I saw those stains, too, Trix, and they *were* paint. Didn't you know that?"

"Then what had he been painting?" Trixie demanded. "I've been thinking and thinking, and I can't remember seeing anything freshly painted, either inside or outside the house—not last night or this afternoon, either."

"That's true," Honey agreed slowly.

Trixie rushed on. "And not only that, but if it *was* Zeke I saw outside the house last night, why didn't he come over and try to help? He could see that Mrs. Franklin was hurt. Why was he listening

161

to us just now? And why is it that, until recently, no one's thought much about Sarah Sligo's ghost? Now, suddenly, everyone's talking about it again. And tell me this. What did the first man die of?"

"Hey, stop!" Honey laughed and held up a protesting hand to stop the string of questions.

Lady seemed to think that her mistress was telling *her* to stop. She flattened her ears back against her head and began slowing to a walk. Honey had to dig her heels gently into the mare's flanks to get her moving again.

As soon as the four horses were cantering abreast once more, Honey asked breathlessly, "What man?"

"The first Lisgard, of course," Trixie said impatiently. "Fay said she heard that he'd wandered off into the marsh and was never seen again. Is that true?"

Di seemed to have been thinking of something else, but now she glanced around at Trixie and grinned. "He didn't die of a bowl of mashed potatoes, if that's what you mean," she said. "I expect he died of old age. After he retired, he turned Lisgard House over to his son and went to live with his married daughter in Massachusetts."

Trixie stared. "Why, Di! How do you know all that?"

Di shrugged her slim shoulders. "There's a book

in the public library that tells about some of the early citizens of Sleepyside. I seem to remember reading about the first Lisgard when I was researching something else. I needed it for an English paper I had to do for school."

Honey was obviously still thinking about Zeke and his paint-stained overalls. "Has Mr. Collins painted anything around the house, Fay?" she asked.

But Fay didn't seem to be particularly interested in Zeke or his strange behavior. Now that they were clattering into the Wheelers' stable yard, she seemed to have the beginnings of that same air of relief about her that Trixie had noticed before.

For the moment, Trixie let the matter drop. The more she thought about the odd-job man, however, the more certain she felt that he knew far more about the strange events at Lisgard House than even Mr. Hunter knew.

I need to talk to Honey alone, Trixie thought to herself as she slid from Susie's broad back. *I haven't even had a chance to tell her about what I saw in Fay's hallway last night.*

A moment later, she realized that she'd had no chance to talk to Di alone, either.

Di's hand on Susie's bridle stopped Trixie from following Honey and Fay as they rode into the

163

warm, fragrant interior of the stable.

"I need to tell you something, Trix," Di said, leaning from her palomino's saddle. "It's the strangest thing. Didn't Fay tell us that Lisgard House was full of genuine antiques?"

Trixie looked up at her, puzzled. "Sure she did. And it *is* full of antiques. You saw them yourself."

Di slowly shook her head. "I saw furniture all right, Trix," she replied, "but it's not what you think. Most of it's fake."

Trixie had no further chance to talk to Di about her astonishing news, for in the next moment, Regan was hurrying toward them.

It was always the same when he realized that his beloved horses had returned safe and sound. He stood over the riders while he made sure that their mounts were groomed and made comfortable. Then he watched to see that the tack was polished and rehung on the stable wall.

This afternoon was no different. Even Di stayed to help, while Sunny waited patiently, knowing his turn would come when he would be led to his own pasture on the Lynch estate.

Trixie had almost finished brushing Susie's sleek black coat when Honey's voice came from the adjoining stall: "If you ask me, Regan's getting worse! He's a real slave driver!"

"I heard that, Honey," Regan's cheerful voice answered from the depths of Strawberry's box, where he was lending Fay a hand. "And let me tell you, if you always did as good a job as your friend here, I wouldn't have to be a slave driver at all."

In another second, both Regan and Fay appeared and stood watching as Trixie hung her bridle neatly on its hook under the saddle peg.

Trixie glanced at them both and noticed that Fay's face looked flushed and happy. "You seem to have been enjoying yourself, Fay," Trixie remarked as she gave her little black mare one last good-bye pat on her shining rump.

"I did enjoy it," Fay said breathlessly. "I'd forgotten what fun it can be—being around horses, I mean. Besides, it helped me to forget—to forget—"

"If it's that much fun," Di's voice floated out to them, "I'll let you help me see to Sunny as soon as I've finished helping Honey."

"Oh, yes!" Fay's voice sounded eager. "That would be great, Di." She hesitated. "That is, if you wouldn't mind, Trixie."

"Of course not!" Trixie sounded more eager than she'd meant to and hoped that Fay hadn't noticed. But she *did* want to talk to Honey alone, and this seemed to be the perfect chance. All the same, she couldn't help feeling some guilt as she added, "Maybe Di would like to show you around her house, too. You'll love it, Fay. It's not a bit spooky—" She broke off, aware that the end of her sentence, *the way your house is*, was already too obvious.

If Mart had been there, he would have told his sister that once more she'd managed to insert her foot firmly into her oral cavity!

Trixie was relieved when she heard Miss Trask's brisk voice call from the stable doorway, "If you're planning a visit to the Lynch house, girls, don't be gone for hours. You're all invited to have supper at Manor House—that is, if you'd like to."

Trixie looked doubtful. "I really think I ought to get home. Moms is going to think I've gotten lost, to say nothing of the chores—"

Miss Trask smiled as she broke in. She was dressed, as usual, in a trim tweed suit, her feet encased in sensible oxfords. "I'm supposed to give you a message, Trixie," she said. "Your parents have taken Bobby to visit Santa in one of Croton's department stores."

Trixie stared. "Santa's come to town *already?*"

Miss Trask's bright blue eyes twinkled. "Would you believe he's been there since last week? Bobby hadn't known about it until Di's twin brothers mentioned it this morning. Now nothing will do but that he has to go and put in his order *at once.*"

Di laughed. "Trust Larry and Terry to tell him about it. I forgot that the nursemaids took them to Ecklund's last Saturday. They had a great time."

Regan grinned at all of them. "I don't know what things are coming to," he said. "It used to be that Santa and his sleigh didn't arrive until Christmas Eve. First came Thanksgiving, and then—"

Miss Trask shook her gray head. "Soon he'll be going out trick-or-treating with the youngsters at Halloween."

"Did you talk to the boys?" Honey asked. "Are they going to eat with us?"

Miss Trask nodded. "They said they wouldn't miss it."

Honey's face brightened. "Will we have hot dogs, Miss Trask? *Dear* Miss Trask?"

Miss Trask laughed aloud as she turned away. "Hot dogs it is, if you really want them."

"Then how can we refuse?" Di sang out. "It all sounds delicious. What do you think, Fay?"

Their new friend had been watching them quietly. Now she smiled and said, "How kind you all are. I don't know how I can ever thank you."

Di flushed. "Come on," she told her quickly. "Let's go and see to Sunny. Then afterward I'll show you around."

"And after that," Fay said happily, "we'll have

hot dogs around a roaring fire!"

They followed Miss Trask out of the stable, and Trixie could hear Fay's light voice sounding once more as if she'd been able to forget her troubles.

Regan hurried away to the back office as Honey stirred and sighed. "I can't help feeling glad that Fay's going to be busy for just a little while, Trix," Honey said. "I've been simply dying to talk to you."

"Me, too," Trixie replied, "because you know what, Honey? I've figured it all out."

Honey stared. "Figured all what out?"

"I've finally figured out what's going on at Lisgard House," Trixie answered simply.

Trixie's Suspicions • 15

ALL RIGHT, TRIX, now tell me all about it," Honey demanded, closing her bedroom door.

Trixie groaned and flung herself into the nearest chair. "Wait up, Honey," she gasped. "You rushed me up here so fast, I haven't had a chance to catch my breath."

She glanced around at her friend's neat room with the crisp, white, ruffled organdy curtains at the windows, a matching bedspread on the comfortable double bed, and a big, white, fluffy rug on the polished floor.

It was such a contrast to the shabby little room they'd shared the previous night, that Trixie realized, once again, what a staunch friend Honey had been to stay there.

"I don't know where to begin," Trixie finally said, uncertainly.

Honey came and perched on the side of the bed. "You can begin by telling me the *real* story about that stupid mouse you said you saw in the hallway last night," she replied. "I could see that Fay believed you, but then, she doesn't know you the way I do. Trixie Belden? Scared of a mouse? That's the silliest thing I ever heard of!"

Trixie grinned at her. "It was the only thing I could think of on the spur of the moment."

Honey leaned toward her. "Well, now you've had time to think about it. And now I want the truth! What was it you saw? It was something that scared the daylights out of you, wasn't it? You should have heard yourself, Trix. I've never heard such a bloodcurdling scream in all my life!"

"Except for the scream we heard later outside Fay's bedroom door," Trixie told her, her face grim. "And I've got an explanation for that, too."

She hesitated, then told Honey everything she knew. Trixie told her about the whispering voice she'd heard when she was alone in the kitchen, after Brian had left the house. She told her of the strange figure she'd seen later, when she had gone to check the lock on the back door.

"It wore a black cloak, Honey," Trixie said slowly. "It had a tall hat on its head. I tried to see its face, but I couldn't. It was in the shadow, somehow. Then, as I looked, its outlines got all faint and wavy. Then it said, 'Beware,' and then it was gone."

Honey's eyes were enormous as they stared at her friend. "Was it the witch's ghost?" she breathed.

"I thought it was," Trixie admitted. "The more I thought about it, you see, the more I realized that I'd been able to see right through it. It was transparent!"

Honey gasped. "Then it *was* the ghost!"

Trixie shook her head. "It was a clever trick to make me think so," she declared. "I almost believed it, too. Then Di told me something, just as we got home this afternoon, that changes everything, Honey! I know what's behind this weird haunting of Lisgard House."

Honey stirred uneasily. "I don't think I understand what you mean, Trix. Mr. Gregory and Mr. Hunter are sure the place really is haunted."

"But it isn't," Trixie said. "You see, there's someone they haven't even thought about. It's someone who's been trying all along to scare everyone away from Lisgard House. And do you know why? Ever since old Caleb died, he's been stealing the antique furniture, Honey. He's had clever fakes made, and he's put them in place of the real stuff. He's been selling that original furniture, probably for pots of money. It's fooled everyone— even Mr. Gregory."

Honey sat back and gasped. "Why—why, Trixie! Who is it you're talking about?"

"Zeke Collins," Trixie announced triumphantly, "that's who!"

"I still don't understand," her friend said, frowning. "I get the bit about the furniture and selling it and everything. But I don't understand at all about any of the other things. Why did he pretend the house was haunted?"

Trixie leaped to her feet as if she couldn't bear to sit still any longer. "Figure it out, Honey. Everything was fine after old Caleb died and after Mr. Gregory moved in. Mr. Gregory wasn't at the house much. He kept on going to New York City on business."

"I get it," Honey said. "That left Zeke with a clear field to do *what* he wanted *when* he wanted. He could remove one piece of furniture and move another back in again in nothing flat. And then, when Mr. Gregory came home again, he never noticed anything, because he isn't an expert on antiques, anyway."

"Exactly," Trixie moved to the windows, pushed aside one of the organdy curtains, and stared out

172

at the gray November landscape.

To her surprise, storm clouds were gathering high overhead, and as she watched, the first gentle drops of rain plopped into the puddles that remained from the storm of two nights before.

"It's raining again," she said to Honey over her shoulder.

But Honey wasn't interested in the weather. "Tell me what Zeke did when the Franklins moved in," she demanded.

Trixie turned from the window. "Zeke must have wondered how he could get rid of them," she said flatly. "Then he had a bright idea. He remembered all the stories that had ever been told about Lisgard House. The ones he didn't remember, he made up. He started spreading rumors and gossip, Honey. It wouldn't have been hard to do. There're always people who are willing to believe that a place is haunted—especially around here in Sleepyside, where everything's so old."

Honey nodded thoughtfully. "Okay. I'm with you, so far. It sounds logical, but—"

"But nothing! Who has a key to just about everything at that house?"

"We don't know that, Trix," Honey objected. "All we know is that he has a key to the front gate."

"I'll bet you he has a key to just about

173

everything else, as well," Trixie replied, "including the back door. Fay told us it worked on a spring lock, remember? She also said it was never bolted, because it could only be opened with a key—Zeke's key!"

Honey tucked her legs under her. "Go on."

Trixie plopped herself back in the chair and ran a hand impatiently through her mop of curls. "If I'm right, Honey," she said slowly, "that means that it was Zeke all along who was causing the 'ghost' to walk. He was the one who kept on opening and closing doors, and moving objects, and blowing out candles—to say nothing about all that other stuff."

Honey was still looking skeptical. "But what about last night, Trix? You still haven't explained last night."

"Tape recorder," Trixie said smugly. "I'll bet it was all done with a tape recorder. Remember that dumb tape Mart's got? One minute it sounds as if a train's rushing right through the middle of the house. And next, it sounds as if the living room's full of barnyard animals. What it is, really, is just a whole lot of sound effects, all—what do you call it?—spliced together. The first time that Mart played it, it scared Moms and me silly."

Honey smiled. "I remember your telling me about that when it happened."

"And that's what Zeke's using—I'm certain of it," Trixie declared. "He could have used the smoke from—from something or other and fanned it under the door in some way. I haven't quite got that worked out yet. As for the figure of that ghost I saw. . . ." She hesitated, as if she hated to speculate.

"Yes, Trix? And what was that?"

"I *think* it was all done with a film projector," Trixie said slowly, "though I'm not sure about that. . . . But I'll bet I'm right about everything else!"

"And what about Mr. Hunter and what happened this afternoon?" Honey asked.

"Zeke used his tape machine again," Trixie answered promptly, "and probably that same fan. This time he used the fan to blow cold air into the room instead of smoke. As for Mr. Hunter, I expect he's worked with spooks so often that he's hearing and seeing them, even where there aren't any at all."

Honey was silent and sat staring at her hands. "Are you going to tell Fay?" she asked at last.

Trixie frowned. "I've been thinking about that, and I've got an idea Fay wouldn't believe it. For too long, she's been living with this thought that she's being taken over by the ghost. It's been several weeks, Honey, and her imagination's been working overtime." She paused. "I've got an idea that Brian's right. If this goes on much longer, Fay's going to need to see a psychiatrist, or something." She clenched her fists. "Ooh, that Zeke! I'd like to see him get what's coming to him!"

Honey looked at her. "I can see how important it is to let Fay know she's not really possessed, after all," she said slowly. "But, Trix, you know we have no proof. None at all!"

"But we do!" Trixie stuck her legs way out in front of her and tapped the sides of her sneakers together thoughtfully. "We have the proof that the antique furniture is fake."

"And that's all we've got," Honey stated. "Even so, Di's not an expert. She could be wrong."

"Then we must tell Mr. Gregory what's been going on," Trixie answered firmly. "He can call in an expert himself. Then, if I were he, I'd send for Sergeant Molinson and then have Zeke Collins arrested."

Honey sighed and got to her feet. "I'm sure you're right, Trix, and it does sound possible that things happened the way you say—"

Trixie stared at her. *"Possible?* But, Honey, it's the *only* way it could have happened! I'm right. I'm just sure of it!"

"Then what do we do now?"

Trixie bit her lip. The truth was that she hadn't worked that out yet.

She wished passionately that her own sensible father hadn't chosen to go to Croton just when she needed him. He could have given her some sound advice.

As she sat there thinking, she had a hunch that he would have told her to be patient—to wait until she was sure of her facts, instead of rushing off impulsively on what could be the wrong track.

On the other hand, Trixie suspected something that her father probably couldn't know: Fay was at the breaking point. Actually, her sanity could be at stake.

Trixie glanced up and found Honey watching her intently.

"We haven't any choice," Trixie said at last. "We've got to get in touch with Mr. Gregory and tell him everything—right now."

The two friends found Miss Trask in the Wheelers' large kitchen. She was helping Cook prepare enormous bowls of potato salad, chips and dips, and olives and pickles, to say nothing of the wieners and buns. A big pot of fragrant soup bubbled gently on the range.

"Has anyone else come yet?" Honey asked, her eyes fixed on the good things to eat.

Miss Trask shook her gray head. "Not yet, dear, but they'll be here soon." She glanced at the kitchen clock. "Supper will be ready in an hour. Are you hungry?"

"We're very hungry," Honey told her, "and everything smells so good. But Trix and I have to go out for a while. We won't be long, honestly. We're just going to grab our bikes and—"

Miss Trask looked surprised as she turned to face them. "Good heavens," she broke in, "it does sound important."

"It is important, Miss Trask," Trixie said breathlessly, "otherwise we'd stay and help. But we—we need to tell someone something. His telephone's supposed to be fixed, but it isn't, so we're just going to take a quick run over there."

Miss Trask never wasted time asking a lot of questions. That was only one of the many things all the Bob-Whites liked about her.

She turned back to the counter where she'd been working and said over her shoulder, "All right, then. But, please, don't be too long."

Trixie hesitated in the kitchen doorway. She noticed it was almost five-thirty. "Are you going to watch the news tonight?" she asked, thinking of Ed Gaffey and his probable report about the haunting of Lisgard House.

Miss Trask didn't even look up. She was busy

slicing onions. "Gracious, Trixie," she said, "I'm sure I'm much too busy to watch television right now. Why do you ask?"

Trixie pretended she hadn't heard the question and let the door close quietly behind her. She could tell from the look on Honey's face that her friend was as relieved as she was.

As soon as they were safely out of the house, Trixie said, "I wonder if Miss Trask would have let us go to Mr. Gregory's if she'd known what happened last night?"

Honey sighed. "I've got a better question, Trix," she said. "I *know* the scary things that happened last night. So why am I going back there with you now?"

"To save a friend," Trixie answered softly, "and—oh, Honey!—I only hope we're not too late."

Strange Behavior! • 16

TRIXIE RACED HOME across the wet grass to grab her bicycle from the garage, while Honey, already mounted on her bike, waited for her patiently at the end of the Beldens' driveway.

It was still drizzling as they sped once more toward Lisgard House, and by the time they reached the mansion's tall front gates, both girls felt wet and uncomfortable.

Trixie wouldn't have been surprised if the reporters and cameramen had still been camped there, hoping to find an opportunity of yet another interview. But there was no one.

It didn't take Trixie long to discover something

else: The gates, which had been so firmly locked before, now opened easily to her touch.

Honey giggled nervously as they wheeled their bikes along the overgrown driveway toward the big front entrance. "What would you have done if we'd been locked out, Trix?" she asked.

"I'd have found a way to get in," Trixie answered confidently, though she had no idea how she would have accomplished it.

It was Mr. Gregory himself who hurried to answer the door. He flung it wide and looked startled when he saw who had been pounding so insistently.

"Why, it's—umm—Trixie Belden and Honey Wheeler, isn't it?" he said. "Perhaps you misunderstood. Mr. Hunter said he'd call you when he was ready to conduct his experiment—"

Trixie could feel her heart pounding with excitement. Now that she was at the point where she had to tell Mr. Gregory that his odd-job man was a crook, she wasn't sure how to begin her story. She glanced desperately around her, as though trying to get some sort of inspiration. But all she saw were the drab walls and the animal heads staring down at her.

She drew a deep breath. "Your furniture's been stolen," she blurted.

Mr. Gregory stared at her. "*What?* What in the

181

world are you talking about, little girl?"

"Oh, I don't blame you for looking so surprised," Trixie rushed on breathlessly. "I—that is, Honey and I—were surprised ourselves when we figured it out."

A sudden movement from the stairs made her stop. She glanced up, and her heart skipped a beat when she noticed a still figure standing there. In the hallway's dim light, the figure looked almost like a ghost. But it was only Mr. Hunter. "What's going on?" he asked.

Mr. Gregory seemed bewildered. Puzzled, he ran a hand through his dark hair. "I'm blessed if I know," he said. "Maybe we'd better talk about it. This way, girls."

He led the way into the living room. This time, Trixie was glad to see, a small fire flickered in the hearth. It did little to warm the room, though neither Mr. Gregory nor Mr. Hunter seemed to notice. Trixie shivered in her damp clothes.

Even while she was trying to marshal her thoughts, Mr. Gregory hurried around the room, turning on lights here and there, as if trying to banish the gloom. Outside, dusk had fallen, and Trixie had a weird idea that someone was watching them through the window.

She turned her head but saw no one.

At last she began to talk, telling Mr. Gregory all

that she had discovered—all that she had guessed—and when she had finished, she looked at the men's serious faces and wondered what they were thinking.

Mr. Gregory stirred. "And you say your friend thinks my furniture isn't genuine?" he asked.

Honey brushed her hair back from her face. "We can't be sure, of course," she said hurriedly, "but our friend, Di, usually knows an awful lot about stuff like that, Mr. Gregory."

Trixie leaned toward him. "In any case, you could easily check it out." She hesitated, then added, "My father's a banker. He'd know whom you could get in touch with to make sure. He'd be glad to help you, I know. Or Honey's father would be glad to come and take a look."

Mr. Hunter said heartily, "It seems to me, Lew, that these young ladies should be congratulated on being so neighborly. It's not everyone who'd have the courage to come and tell the story we've just heard."

Mr. Gregory was silent. It was as if he hadn't quite managed to get over the shock of Trixie's news. "I just can't believe it," he muttered. "Zeke Collins! After all these years of working for my uncle! It seems incredible!"

"Not only that," Trixie declared impulsively, "but it means this house isn't haunted, after all.

Don't you see? Fay Franklin *wasn't* a channel for any old witch's ghost. It was Zeke Collins who was trying to scare the Franklins away."

Mr. Hunter's fingers formed their steeple once more, and he nodded slowly. "It's possible," he muttered, as if to himself. "Yes, it's possible that I could have been mistaken."

"Would you, please, tell Fay that you could have made a mistake?" Trixie asked eagerly. "She's been so worried about this whole thing, you see—"

Mr. Hunter looked up suddenly, as if he'd just come to a decision. "Of course I'll tell her," he said. "Bring her here tonight. About nine o'clock, I think. Is that all right with you, Lew?" He glanced quickly at Mr. Gregory.

"Yes, of course," Mr. Gregory answered, but he sounded as if he were thinking about something else. Then, suddenly, he seemed to realize it. "I just can't get over it," he explained. "But, of course, you bring young Fay here at nine. I'll be glad to see you, and we can talk some more. In the meantime, I'm going to have a long talk with Zeke. That man's got a lot of explaining to do. You leave it to me, okay?"

Trixie felt so relieved, once she and Honey were standing outside again, that she didn't even notice the gray sky or feel the rain beating harder and harder now against her bare head.

She didn't notice the raindrops trickling down the back of her neck until she and Honey were almost to the front gate. Then she shook her head vigorously, just the way Reddy shook himself when he was wet.

"Jeepers!" she exclaimed. "Am I hungry! I can't wait to get at those yummy hot dogs. And wait till I tell the others about this!"

"Not so fast!" a rough voice said. "First, you're going to tell me!" A large hand reached out and grabbed Trixie's arm.

Trixie gasped. Her bicycle, suddenly released from her nerveless hand, crashed sideways to the ground, its wheels spinning. The relentless grip on her arm tightened.

She caught one glimpse of Honey's white face as she stared over Trixie's shoulder.

"Oh, Trixie!" Honey breathed, one hand over her horrified mouth. "It's Zeke Collins!"

Afterward, Trixie was never proud of what she did next, even though her reaction was instinctive.

She wrenched her arm free, turned on her heel, and ran madly for the front gate, leaving her bike on the wet grass behind her.

In another moment, she was racing homeward as fast as she could go, her heart pounding, her breath sobbing in her throat, and her legs pumping as fast as if she were in a race.

Then soon—too soon—she heard the sound of bicycle wheels singing toward her along the wet road.

Trixie wished with all her heart that she hadn't left her bike behind for her pursuer to use. But it was too late! Those singing tires were gaining on her—there wasn't any doubt of it.

She tried to summon an extra burst of speed, but by now her tired legs refused to obey her terrified brain. Suddenly she knew she was defeated.

She stopped, trembling, bending double, her hand pressed to the pain in her side, and struggling for breath. She waited to feel the rough hand grab her arm. She waited to hear the rough voice demanding an explanation, even though an explanation wasn't necessary. She knew without question that Zeke Collins had stood outside that living room window, had eavesdropped, and had heard her accusations.

She closed her eyes.

"Brother!" Honey's voice said behind her. "I thought I'd never catch up with you, Trix! I've never seen anyone run so fast in my life! I had to pedal like crazy even to get close. Didn't you hear me calling you? Are you all right? I'll bet you've broken the record for running the mile in two seconds flat. You aren't hurt, are you?"

Trixie opened her eyes and was relieved to see Honey's concerned face bending toward her. "Where's Zeke Collins?" Trixie said in a croaking voice.

"Is that who you thought was chasing you?" Honey gasped. "Oh, Trix! I'm sorry I scared you." She waved a hand in the direction of Lisgard House. "He's back there somewhere. I've never seen anyone look as surprised as he did when you took off like that."

Trixie still struggled to catch her breath. "Where—where's my bike?" she panted.

Honey's face was rueful. "I'm afraid it's still where you left it," she answered. "I was so busy getting out of there myself that I didn't stop for anything."

It took Trixie a few more moments before she was ready to continue on the journey home with Honey. "I expect he'll sell it," she said gloomily. "He's already sold just about everything else."

"You mean Zeke?" Honey asked thoughtfully. "Oh, I don't know, Trix. Somehow I don't think he'd be interested in an old bike. But I wonder what's going to happen now? Will Mr. Gregory call the police?"

With Honey content to pedal her bike at Trixie's side, they turned into the Wheelers' driveway.

"I hope Zeke Collins gets everything that's coming to him," Trixie muttered, watching Honey store her bike back in its proper place in the spacious garage.

"I hope so, too," Honey said. "And, oh, Trix, don't you feel glad? Once Mr. Hunter explains everything to Fay tonight, the case will be closed at last."

Trixie didn't answer. As she followed her friend into Manor House, she had a sudden feeling that maybe Fay wasn't going to be as easy to convince as Honey thought she was.

An hour later, Trixie had managed to throw off her feelings of gloom and doom as she sat with Fay and the rest of the Bob-Whites in the Wheelers' large and formal dining room.

Her eyes twinkled as she looked across the gleaming table at Honey and Mart, who had been arguing the merits of the school's Thanksgiving play.

"With my brains and Brian and Jim's colossal talents," Mart was saying, "the entire affair will, without a doubt, establish us as thespians forevermore. In fact—" he paused and tried to look modest—"we are momentarily expecting a call from Tinsel Town—that's Hollywood, Trix—begging us to depart for that noble city forthwith."

"But, honestly," Honey protested, "don't you think the story of Miles Standish and Priscilla has been done to death? Why, I remember we were doing that same old thing in kindergarten!"

"Ah, but never like this," Mart declared.

"I'll bet!" Trixie couldn't resist adding. She laughed when she caught sight of Mart's indignant face.

Mart was obviously still trying to think of a crushing reply when Brian leaned forward and asked, "How come you haven't told us anything about what you girls have been up to this afternoon? Did you get your clothes okay, Fay?"

"Yes, I've been wondering about that, too," Jim said. "What happened, Trix?"

Trixie bit her lip and hesitated. She almost wished that Fay weren't present to hear about the exciting conclusions she'd reached. Would Fay believe that the frightening things that had been happening to her these past weeks had been caused by one greedy man?

I'll have to make it sound very *convincing*, Trixie thought as she began her story.

The Bob-Whites listened in silence as Trixie told them everything that had happened from the time they'd arrived at Lisgard House that afternoon until she and Honey left it that evening.

She finished and glanced apprehensively at

Fay, who was sitting quiet and still, her hands in her lap.

Suddenly Fay pushed back her chair and stood up. "I don't believe it!" she cried. "It couldn't have happened that way at all!"

Startled, Dan raised his dark head and stared at her. "Hey, hold on!" he exclaimed. "I thought you'd be pleased to hear Trixie's theory. It's possible she's right, you know. She often is."

Fay shook her head. "But not this time! No! Not this time. *I just know it!*"

She sounded so vehement that Trixie frowned. All at once, all her old suspicions about this new friend of theirs came flooding back. Was Fay playing some strange game of her own? If so, what could it be?

It wasn't until they had pushed back their chairs and were leaving the room that Mart made his incredible suggestion. He put his hand on Trixie's arm and whispered in her ear, "Are you thinking what I'm thinking, Trix? Has it occurred to you that maybe Zeke Collins isn't the thief at all?"

Trixie gasped. "Then who could it be?"

"Haven't you guessed?" Mart said quietly. "It's the Franklins, of course!"

Return to Lisgard House · 17

TRIXIE'S THOUGHTS were still in a whirl as she followed her friends slowly into Honey's living room.

She glanced up at the ornate clock that sat in the middle of the Wheelers' mantelpiece. Eight-thirty! In another few minutes, it would be time to leave for Lisgard House. Already the boys were insisting that they were going to accompany the girls.

"There's no way you're going to leave us behind," Mart announced firmly, even though no one was arguing with him. "If Zeke is the dirty-deed-doer—and I *did* say *if*—he could try to camouflage himself as an antique hat rack or something and try to kidnap the lot of you."

"What's that about Zeke?" Miss Trask's brisk voice asked as she hurried into the room. "What's that old rascal been up to now? By the way, Trixie, he was just here."

Trixie leaped to her feet, startled. "Here?" she gasped. "He was here?"

Miss Trask frowned at the note of panic in her voice. "He brought your bike back, though how he knew you were here and not at home is more than I can imagine."

But I know, Trixie thought. *He must have followed us, after all.*

Trixie swallowed hard. "Has he gone?" she asked and discovered she was trembling. She had a horrible suspicion that Zeke was lurking out there in the dark somewhere. He was waiting to pounce on her as soon as she set foot outside the front door. She noticed that Miss Trask was staring at her thoughtfully.

"Oh, yes, he's gone," Miss Trask said, "but I can see that you're upset about something. The condition seems to be catching. Zeke Collins was upset about something, too. He wouldn't tell me what it was. If you ask me, I think he's beginning to believe his own stories. I told him so."

"And what did he say?" Mart asked.

Miss Trask smiled. "To be honest, I didn't let him say anything, Mart. I simply gave him a piece of my mind. I could see for myself how much his ridiculous ghost stories had frightened Fay. I told him in no uncertain terms that he had no business going around scaring honest people out of their wits. Him and his silly tombstone! Witches and ghosts! Great heavens! I've never heard such nonsense."

Trixie's mind seemed suddenly to have snapped to attention. "What do you mean, silly tombstone?" she asked. "What is so silly about a tombstone?"

"Nothing at all, if it's a genuine one," Miss Trask answered promptly. "But if it's Sarah Sligo's tombstone we're talking about—and we are—then that's another matter. I know for a fact that Zeke Collins made it himself."

Trixie gasped. "Then that *isn't* the witch's grave—where the headstone is, I mean?"

"Of course not," Miss Trask said briskly. "No one ever found out where Sarah Sligo was buried."

Brian stirred. "And did she die on Thanksgiving night?"

"Oh, yes, that's common knowledge. But no one can be sure when she was born, or where she was born, for in those days it was unusual for any kind of record to be kept." Miss Trask turned to leave.

193

"Jim tells me you're going out, Honey. As you youngsters *will* be all together, I won't worry about you. Don't be late, however."

There was silence after the door had closed quietly behind her. Then everyone began talking at once.

"So Trixie *was* right!" Dan exclaimed.

"It *was* Zeke who was spreading all those rumors about the witch!" Di added.

Brian climbed to his feet. "Good for you, Trixie!" he said warmly.

"It really looks as if Ms. Sherlock Belden has struck again!" Mart put in.

Then everyone laughed as Jim gave Trixie the thumb's-up sign from across the room. The Bob-Whites guessed that even if Trixie's theories turned out to be incorrect, Jim would still believe that everything she did was right.

Trixie could feel her face getting red. She was about to smile back at him, when all at once she noticed something else.

The large portrait of Honey's mother hung over the fireplace. Blond and frail, Mrs. Wheeler was smiling at Trixie, too.

Trixie stood looking up at her. Suddenly she remembered Lisgard House as she had last seen it. She remembered the overgrown bushes outside the living room windows where Zeke must have crouched, listening. She remembered the mansion's interior, with its gloomy walls and stuffed animal heads. She remembered the antique furniture—all of it fake. *Something had been missing— something important. . . .*

Then suddenly, she knew everything!

She heard Mart exclaim, "Watch out, Brian! Methinks our sibling's gone off into a daydream!"

Then Honey's voice said, "Trix? Is anything wrong?"

To Honey's astonishment, Trixie didn't answer right away. She raced for the door—and only then she turned to gaze at the startled faces turned toward her.

"Oh, don't you see?" she cried impatiently. "Everything's wrong, and there isn't a minute to lose! Quick, Honey! I've got to use your phone!"

Five minutes later, Trixie was leaning forward in the front seat of the big station wagon, as if to urge it to go faster. With Jim at the wheel, the car sped toward Lisgard House with its load of puzzled passengers.

"Would someone mind telling me what's going on?" Mart demanded from his seat behind his sister.

"Whatever's going on," Brian remarked, "we won't get there at all if Jim doesn't slow down."

"There *is* a speed limit along here, Jim," Dan put in. "It would be too bad if we got a ticket."

"Especially with the Bob-White treasury flat broke at the moment," Di said, laughing.

"What I want to know," Mart put in, "is which of our many acquaintances did Trixie call?"

Trixie didn't seem to be listening, and Fay sat quiet, as intent on the road as Trixie was.

The rain had stopped as quickly as it had begun, though the very air around them was hushed, as if the storm were waiting only for the right moment to begin again.

Trixie could hear nothing but the tires singing on the wet road and the purr of the powerful engine under the car's long hood.

"This is it," Jim muttered, pulling up in front of the entrance gates. "I wonder if we should go in this way or around the back?"

Trixie didn't wait for Fay to answer. Already she had scrambled out of the car and flung the gates open. When the station wagon had passed through, she swung them shut and jumped back into her seat once more.

She peered toward the dark mass that was the front of Lisgard House. She couldn't help wondering what Mr. Gregory was going to say when he discovered he was about to receive more visitors than he'd invited.

It was a question that was soon answered. Mr. Gregory seemed taken aback for only a moment when he saw the group of young people standing at his front door. Then he flung the door wide.

"Come in," he said heartily. "I'm glad to see you. I'm glad you brought your friends, Fay, my dear. The more the merrier."

Still talking, he led the way into the living room, where he stood, smiling at them.

"We hope you don't mind us all being here," Honey said breathlessly after she'd made the introductions, "but the boys insisted on coming with us, and—" She glanced quickly around the room. "But where's Mr. Hunter?"

"He's here," Mr. Gregory answered. He walked slowly to the study door and flung it open.

Trixie heard Fay gasp as she and her friends crowded at the room's entrance.

The study walls had been hung with some kind of floating black draperies. Flickering candles stood on every available surface. A table in the room's center wore a black velvet cloth. At its head sat Mr. Hunter.

He wore a dark cloak. His long, thin fingers held a crystal ball. His face, in the flickering candlelight, looked solemn and, Trixie thought, completely confident.

He rose to his feet as soon as he saw the visitors.

For one brief moment, Trixie saw that he, too, looked surprised when he saw how many there were. In the next instant, however, his face was once more a mask of polite welcome as Fay nervously introduced each Bob-White in turn.

Then she said, her voice trembling, "What—what is all this?" She glanced around the small study, where tall shadows reached to the ceiling.

Mr. Gregory frowned as he turned to Trixie. "I want you to know how much I appreciated your coming to me this afternoon," he began, "and I also want you to know that I've had a long talk with Zeke Collins."

Trixie could feel her heart pounding with excitement. "Yes?" she said. "And what did he say?"

Mr. Gregory's face looked grim. "He confessed everything," he said simply. "But I'm afraid it wasn't quite what you suspected, Trixie. You see, the man's a painter—an artist, I mean. All these years, he's been painting what you might say is a monument to Lisgard House."

Mart stammered. "A monument? What kind of monument?"

Mr. Gregory sighed. "He's been painting pictures—beautiful pictures—on the walls of his cottage. He showed me." He paused. "He had an idea that one day the Sleepyside Historical Society would want to preserve that cottage as a museum. It was his gift to society, you might say."

"I still don't understand," Di said bluntly.

"He had an idea that when old Caleb died and I took over," Mr. Gregory went on, "I was going to sell the house and the grounds—everything."

"And weren't you?" Brian demanded.

Mr. Gregory smiled ruefully. "I did have some idea of doing so at one time," he said slowly. "But then I discovered I liked it here. In any case, Zeke had already begun his campaign of rumor and gossip about the house being haunted. And so, you see, no one would have bought it, anyway."

"Was he afraid that if you sold the house and grounds that he'd be out of a job?" Dan asked.

"Not only that," Mr. Gregory said, "but he knew that his cottage would have to be sold as well. He was certain that no one would want either him or his work."

"But he couldn't have been sure of that," Honey objected.

"I'm only telling you how Zeke felt," Mr. Gregory replied. "As to the business with the furniture"—he glanced quickly at Di—"he flatly denies knowing anything about it. He's sure there's been some kind of mistake. He's equally sure that the house *is* genuinely haunted. He believes that something he has done—or someone else has done—" he didn't look at Fay—"has called the witch from her grave, wherever that may be. Oh, yes—" he nodded his head—"Zeke has told me all about the fake headstone."

"And that's why," Mr. Hunter put in quickly, "we must lay Sarah to rest once and for all. If we don't, there's no telling what's going to happen. The spirit is an evil one, you see. And so we must conduct a seance. *Now. Tonight*. We simply *must* send Sarah back to—to that other plane we call death." He glanced at Fay. "My dear, you told me this afternoon that you'd help us." He took her hand. "Are you still willing? With my powers, joined to yours, we must succeed."

Trixie held her breath and watched as Fay, as if in a dream, walked slowly to the table and sat down. "I knew this was going to happen all along," Fay said simply, "and I'm ready."

"I'll bet she's ready," Trixie heard Mart whisper in her ear. "Can't you see, Trix? She's ready to confess. I'm sorry to say this, but now we know for sure your friend's a thief!"

Sarah Sligo's Revenge • 18

MOMENTS LATER, the Bob-Whites were seated at the velvet-covered table, their hands joined. A lighted candelabra, set on a small table at Fay's elbow, threw shadows across her pale face as Mr. Hunter took his place beside her. Trixie could see Mr. Gregory, on Fay's other side, gripping her hand reassuringly.

Fay's nervous, Trixie thought, *and she has good reason to be!*

"Is everyone ready?" Mr. Hunter asked. As heads nodded, he said, "Then let's begin."

Trixie was fascinated as she watched this strange man breathe deeply, as if he were doing

201

some kind of psychic exercise. Then, all at once, he let out his breath in one long sigh, his head sank to his chest, and a long moan escaped from his lips.

"Are you there, Sarah?" he asked in a husky voice that didn't sound like his own.

Unbelievably, there came the whispered answer, "I am here! *And now for my revenge!*"

Everything seemed to happen at once. A violent wind rushed into the room. It set the candles to flickering wildly. The flimsy black draperies reached toward them. Someone's elbow moved sharply, and in another instant, the tall candelabra crashed to the floor. The flames from those candles joined with the others. Then, while the Bob-Whites watched, too horrified to move, the curtains caught fire.

Fay screamed and jumped to her feet as a wall of fire licked quickly to the ceiling. "It's the witch!" she cried. "She's here—in this room! Oh, please! Make her stop!"

Mr. Hunter seemed to come awake with a start. "It's too late to stop her now," he said sadly. "I'm sorry, but Sarah's evil spirit was too powerful for both of us, Fay. I'm afraid the witch has won! She's set the house on fire, just as I was afraid she would. Nothing can save it now!"

"Except the fire department," Trixie said as,

with the others, she rushed outside to the safety of the grounds.

"We can't call the fire department!" Mr. Gregory cried. "It's too late! The old house is a goner!" Then he stopped as he heard what Trixie had been hearing for the last two minutes: A fire engine's siren wailed as it came closer and closer to Lisgard House.

"But—but that's impossible!" Mr. Hunter exclaimed as he watched the fire truck scream through the wide gates, which stood open, waiting for it.

"But it isn't impossible at all," Trixie told the astonished man. "You see, *I* made the arrangements for the fire department to be called even before we arrived here tonight."

Jim gasped. "You mean you *knew* what was going to happen tonight?"

"Then *was* it Zeke Collins who's been causing all the trouble?" Di asked.

Trixie shook her head and stared at the silent figure of Mr. Gregory. "No," she told the Bob-Whites, "it wasn't Zeke—and it wasn't the Franklins, either. Oh, don't you see? It was Mr. Gregory himself!"

A few days later, Trixie and her friends were gathered in Mrs. Franklin's hospital room. Even

Zeke Collins, looking a bit sheepish, was there.

Fay was radiant. As her mother kept repeating over and over, she looked like a different girl.

"That's because I *am* a different girl," Fay told her, laughing. "No one knows what it was like believing that I was possessed by a ghost!"

"I blame myself," Zeke blurted. "If I hadn't, like a blamed fool, started all those ghost stories—"

"—which you began to believe yourself," Dan told him sternly.

"Begin at the beginning and tell us all about it again, Trix," Honey said, smiling.

Trixie sat on a corner of Mrs. Franklin's bed. "It all began when Mr. Gregory inherited that big old house," she said. "But he had no money, so he tried to sell it."

"But no one would buy," Brian put in, "once Zeke told them his made-up history of the place."

"Though part of it was true," Mart objected. "Sarah Sligo really had lived there once. And she really *did* die a violent death—"

"And it was the ghost stories that gave Lewis Gregory his idea," Trixie went on. "He decided to have Sarah 'haunt' the place again. Then, when the time was right, he was going to burn it down in order to collect the insurance money. Fay had already told us that the place and its contents were well insured. But Gregory needed witnesses who could back up his story of how the fire started. He'd already begun replacing the real antique furniture with the fake stuff, of course, by this time. And then he hired Mrs. Franklin. He paid her a high salary so she wouldn't leave."

"How foolish I was," Mrs. Franklin sighed.

"But you couldn't have known what he had in mind," Fay said quickly.

"And when Mr. Gregory thought the time was right," Trixie continued, "he hired Mr. Hunter, who really *was* a psychic investigator—but a crooked one."

"And when Gregory offered to pay him well for his services," Jim put in, "Hunter agreed to help. He was prepared to swear in court that the house was genuinely haunted and that evil spirits can prey on the living—in this case, Fay Franklin."

Trixie nodded. "Yes. Once the two crooks saw the effect the ghostly happenings were having on Fay, they got the idea of blaming her for starting the fire that night. They put the lighted candles right by her elbow. They hoped they could scare her so much that *she'd* be the one who would make those draperies catch on fire. All of us—" she smiled at the Bob-Whites—"would also be witnesses then that Fay, 'possessed' by Sarah, had burned the house down to the ground."

"And it might have worked," Fay said softly.

"His plan was almost stopped before it began," Trixie said, "when Mrs. Franklin broke her hip. Lewis Gregory hadn't meant for that to happen. *He* was the one I saw outside the mansion when we first arrived at Lisgard House. It wasn't Zeke at all. Gregory had almost overreached himself that night. What made you fall, Mrs. Franklin? Did you hear strange noises?"

Mrs. Franklin nodded. "I heard footsteps upstairs, and I knew it wasn't Fay."

Brian stirred. "He must have thought his best witness was gone for good," he said, "when the ambulance took her to the hospital."

"But then," Honey broke in, "he realized he could go ahead with the frightening climax to the 'haunting,' after all—"

"Because you and Trixie agreed to spend the night with me," Fay said breathlessly. "Boy, I'll never forget what happened then."

"He let himself in through the back door," Trixie continued, "to which he also had a key. He used a tape machine to provide all the sound effects, just as I suspected—"

"And he used my smudge pots," Zeke said. "He must have got them from my greenhouse. I use them to stop plants from freezing in the cold weather."

"And with a fan," Trixie said, "he blew the

smoke under Fay's bedroom door."

Mart frowned. "I still don't understand something," he declared. "Why didn't Gregory just incinerate Lisgard House and tell everyone that it must have been kids playing with matches?"

Di looked surprised. "Didn't I tell you? Sergeant Molinson has found out that Gregory had already used that story before."

Honey gasped. "I didn't know that!"

"It was a warehouse that was burned several years ago," Di told her. "Gregory had a partner in those days, and it was the partner who was suspected of setting the fire then. But the police think Lewis Gregory didn't dare tell the same story twice, so that's why he dreamed up another scheme instead."

"And I would have been blamed for the Lisgard House fire," Fay remarked, shivering.

"And we might not have been able to save you," Dan put in. "*I* wasn't sure who knocked over the candles at that seance."

"But *I* know," Trixie said. "Once I suspected what was going to happen, I watched Lewis Gregory all the time. It was *his* elbow that knocked over the candelabra."

Mrs. Franklin sighed. "Just think," she said. "If Trixie hadn't seen Mrs. Wheeler's portrait when she did, Gregory might have been successful!"

Jim grinned. "I still don't understand how Mom's portrait helped our girl sleuth figure everything out."

Trixie laughed. "I looked at it," she said, "and I thought of the Picasso. Then I remembered it wasn't in the hall when we went back to get Fay's clothes. Mr. Gregory had taken it down. I wondered why. Then I thought about that headstone. Miss Trask had said it was fake. But Hunter, who was supposed to be an expert, had agreed at once with Zeke's story that a spirit who had died on its birthday couldn't rest. I realized then that everything I'd suspected about Zeke could apply to Mr. Gregory, especially if Hunter was a crook. I think that at one time, Gregory intended to set fire to the house on Thanksgiving night—to fit the story. Then he must have decided he couldn't wait, especially when we found out about the fake furniture. So he decided to act sooner. The picture of the blue clown was the only thing in the house he liked. And he sure didn't want it to burn in the fire he intended to start *that night*, in front of witnesses."

Mart laughed. "And Trixie didn't call the fire department; she had someone else do it for her. Neat!"

Mrs. Franklin looked bewildered. "Then whom did she call? I don't understand. I've been wondering who would believe her suspicions."

"I called the only person who might be vitally interested in saving Lisgard House," Trixie said simply. "I called Zeke Collins. He believed me at once."

"Everything Trixie told me made sense," Zeke explained, "and so I called the fire chief and told him to stand by. Him and me are old buddies, so luckily he did what I asked him to."

Fay sighed. "What's going to happen now?"

"The Historical Society has seen Mr. Collins's work," Di said. "We've seen it, too. The paintings in the cottage are beautiful, and the Society is determined to save them."

"As for Lisgard House," Honey said, "parts of the downstairs were badly burned in the fire. But a group of local businessmen, including my dad, and Di's dad, are going to repair it and buy it and turn it over to the Society. Zeke is going to be kept on as artist in residence. Isn't that great?"

"And Lewis Gregory?" Fay asked. "What about him? Is he going to jail?"

Trixie nodded. "Sergeant Molinson is sure of it. The insurance company is going to sue him for fraud, you see. Mr. Hunter will go to jail with him."

"And now we have a surprise for you, Mrs. Franklin," Honey said, laughing. "Di's father has found you another job—on a lovely ranch, with lots of horses, Fay. What's more, the insurance company is paying us a reward for saving Lisgard House."

"And the Bob-Whites want you to have the money for Fay's education," Trixie added happily.

Mrs. Franklin's eyes filled with tears. "We don't know how to thank you all," she said.

"Especially Trixie," Fay added.

"Just have the best Thanksgiving ever," Trixie said, feeling so thankful herself that this strange mystery was solved at last.

As she watched the happy group around Mrs. Franklin's bed, she suddenly remembered the strange figure who had twice warned her to be careful. Lewis Gregory had now flatly denied doing so. *Who had it been?* Had the real whispering witch been doing her best to protect what had once been her earthly home?

Later, as the Bob-Whites were on their way home, Trixie saw once more the tall outlines of Lisgard House.

She rolled down her car window and whispered to the still air around it, "You can rest now, Sarah."

And she had a sudden feeling that she'd been heard.